"This anthology already made its reputation with *Unthank* as a display of the new fiction coming from UEA's Creative Writing course from which many leading writers have emerged. This new anthology celebrates the work – lively, varied and fresh – of the new group of writers whose promise looks just as good as before. Here you'll find several new writers you will certainly want to read again, and a sense of the rising promise of new fiction from an international group."

MALCOLM BRADBURY

"The Creative Writing MA at East Anglia draws new fiction-writers from around the world. In 1990, for example, they come from New Zealand, Canada and Iceland as well as Britain, to share their energies, pool their nightmares, and discover how very diverse their individual styles are. This anthology celebrates that vital variety, and bears witness to our local paradox – a continuing tradition of making it new."

LORNA SAGE

exposure
fiction from the workshop

exposure
fiction from the workshop

introduced by Rose Tremain
with a foreword by
Ian McEwan

Edited by
Philip McCann
Editor-in-chief
Jon Cook

CCPA

Published in 1991
by the Centre for Creative and Performing Arts,
University of East Anglia,
Norwich, England

Printed and bound in Great Britain by
University of East Anglia
Set in Goudy Old Style

British Library Cataloguing in Publication Data
Exposure: fiction from the Workshop
1. Fiction in English. 1945– Anthologies
I. McCann, Philip 1963–
823.91408
ISBN 0 9515009 1 0

acknowledgements

Thankful acknowledgement is made to the Eastern Arts
Association for financial assistance.

This second anthology published by the Centre for
Creative and Performing Arts was made possible through
the cooperation of the Norfolk Institute of Art and Design.
We should like to thank Andy Vargo and Mike Oakes for
their expert help and guidance, and Anna Scher for
permission to quote the motto of the Anna Scher Theatre
in Islington. Jon Cook's editorial expertise is much
appreciated, as is the advice of Gerri Brightwell.

The line 'Oh gride on and dremmer, glem so and durb!' in
Refrain on page 65, is taken from *The Bolham's Replover:
Farewell to Jabberwocky* by Hugh Haughton published in
The Chatto Book of Nonsense Poetry © Hugh Haughton
1988 (Chatto and Windus). The publishers would like to
thank the author and publishing house for permission to
quote from the above.

foreword
by Ian McEwan

I graduated from the University of Sussex in the summer of 1970. I had already written three quite useless plays, but writing, 'being' a writer, was still a vague and intensely private ambition. I had a clearer notion that the last thing I wanted was regular employment, and that it would therefore be a good idea to remain a student. I had a graduate grant for one year. I was convinced that my life had not yet begun. I wanted to be in a town where no one knew me. But I squandered the summer in northern Italy, doing nothing about finding a university, and it was not until September that I phoned the University of East Anglia. In those days, or at that particular moment, it was the easiest thing to be put through to Professor Malcolm Bradbury. I explained that I had read of a new MA which allowed, in one component, fiction to be submitted in place of a written dissertation. He explained that no one had applied and the course had never got off the ground. I suggested that my phone call was a sort of application. He suggested that I send him my fiction. I had none. For the next two weeks I sat in the bedroom of my parents' house in Middle Wallop and while my sunburn flaked wrote two short stories. I remember nothing of them beyond my assumption that single spaced typing looked somehow more serious.

I count the year I spent in Norwich from October 1970 as the luckiest, most productive in my life. My sixties began. I made important, enduring friendships, and some tortuous transient ones. I met my future wife. I discovered the north Norfolk coast. I took mescalin. I experimented with alcohol. In a rented room on the Newmarket Road, and later, in a terraced house on Silver Road, I wrote stories, and thrilled myself with the romance of writing into the dawn, and on into the late morning. I thought my life had begun. When I had work to show, I met Malcolm in his office or in the Maid's Head. He was a liberal and practical critic, and he made me feel free. He was happy to let me go my own way. I never revised my stories, but I tried to incorporate the spirit of his suggestions in whatever came next. I was drawn to his sense of humour, which I found immensely tolerant, and I think there were times when I wrote to it. I certainly did for a story of mine called *Homemade*.

In the spring term came Angus Wilson. The pink face floating above a white suit was the living emblem of the strawberry and champagne garden parties for which he was celebrated among his students. An opulent glow surrounded him and his friend Tony Garret. It was a strange light from another world – pre-war, upper middle class, bohemian, dandified, mischievous – and it shone out against the Lasdun concrete. From Angus and Tony I understood what it could mean to perform in, to be classy in, conversation. They were great collectors of people; their gaiety was never merely sexual, and they never forgot a student's name. Angus had a particular penchant for hippy girls. He liked to exclaim loudly and fuss over their bangles and pendants. He and Tony would happily come and sit on the floor of a student flat and perform. They would even listen, and remember. I am not certain that Angus ever said much to me about my stories, except to tick me off once for homophobia, and to imply that I was to inherit the nastiness of his *Strawberry Jam*. He was the reader I had in mind when I wrote a story called *Disguises*. He seemed to think I was already a writer. He once introduced me to his publisher as one and I felt a fraud. When I came back to Norwich after a long absence in Kabul, I slipped into one of his seminars. Without breaking stride he waved me into a chair – *Dear boy, we must get you some Arts Council money,* (he was Chairman at the time) *how lean and brown you are, now Dickens was already treating the anti-Americanism of his predecessors as something of a racket . . .*

The first writer in residence at UEA was Alan Burns, and he came in the summer of 1971. He was a lawyer who had written some critically successful experimental novels that were not widely read. I have the impression that his time in Norwich turned his life around: he gave up the law and became a creative writing teacher. He spent a lot of time with my work. He warned me of the dangers of being influenced by writers whom I had not read. He gave me Beckett's early fiction, *More Pricks than Kicks*, and the trilogy. I saw what he meant. I was becoming enslaved to cadences whose origins I did not know. It was a useful warning.

At the end of the year, Malcolm sent one of my stories to *Transatlantic Review* and it was accepted. By then I had written most of the stories that were to make up the volume *First Love, Last Rites*. More than any lesson, or the benefit of a 'course', had been the simple fact of having been taken seriously. During the seventies the UEA course established itself. I do not know how I would have got on in the tougher, more paranoid milieu of twelve or fifteen competitive colleagues. I might well have faded out, and this was the extent of my luck in 1970 – to have had it all to myself. I am certain though that the value of Malcolm Bradbury's Creative Writing MA remains unchanged: to be given serious attention is all a new writer can demand, and publication in this volume is one more version of that.

Ian McEwan
Oxford July 1990

talent thrives on training together

Anna Scher

contents

Introduction

I t is now almost twenty years since the MA Course in Creative Writing was set up by Angus Wilson and Malcolm Bradbury at the University of East Anglia. Ian McEwan was its founder student in 1970 and the following year the first small group of writers assembled for the three hour weekly workshops that are the focal point of the course. The popularity of this MA (confirmed this year by one thousand enquiries and almost two hundred applications for the ten available places) is due in large measure to its proven ability to attract young writers who go on to become internationally known. The notion that it exists as a kind of bridge from obscurity to fame is certainly present in the minds of many applicants. This, however, is to ask of it rewards that it cannot necessarily deliver. Its promises are these: it takes the beginning writer out of an unhelpful and sometimes destructive isolation and provides him with a peer group whose hopes and fears are similar to his own; it places his work under the kind of scrutiny that reveals where its weaknesses lie and where its strengths; and, above all, it helps him to understand that great writing does not rest only on what Malcolm Bradbury has called innocent inspiration, but also upon skills and techniques that can be studied and acquired.

The work in this anthology has been written by the nine MA students participating in the 1989-1990 course, with an additional contribution from Rolf Hughes who was a member of the 1988-89 MA group and who has stayed on at UEA to complete his Ph.D in Creative and Critical Writing. Having published a story last year, Rolf, then, is the only one of these writers whose prose fiction has already faced exposure. It is a significant moment in any writer's life: the traumatic passage of the work from private to public ownership, from containable scrutiny to mass attention. It is my belief that, just as Art School graduates have their Degree Show and Drama School students their Final Production to initiate them into the process of exposure, so it is helpful to writers about to become supplicants at the doors of agents and publishers to have their best work put before a critical readership. That said, it is important to point out that the idea for an anthology came neither from Malcolm nor from me, but from two of last years students, Gerri Brightwell and Mark Slater. This year, in conjunction with UEA's Centre for Creative and Performing Arts (CCPA) and with the Norfolk Institute of Art and Design, it is Philip McCann who designs the book and, with Robert Whittaker, sees it through from the first to the last phase of its production.

Last year's anthology, *Unthank*, sold a thousand copies. It is my expectation that those sale figures will be increased this year and that in the game so loved by publishers called Hunt the Successful Writer of Tomorrow, it will come to be one of the first places the editors will look.

This year's MA group is one of the most interestingly disparate, in terms of age, nationality and preoccupation we have had in recent years. We have students from Iceland, Canada, New Zealand and Ireland, Wilhelm Emilsson, Michelle Heinemann, Judy Corbalis and Philip McCann, and we have two mature students, Nairne Plouviez and John Wakeman who have come late to fiction after substantial careers in teaching and editing. John Wakeman's contribution is an extract from a picaresque novel-in-progress about the protagonist's relationship with Edward James (1907-1985), renowned collector of surrealist art and a putative bastard of King Edward VII. Another novel extract comes from Rolf Hughes. His *Refrain* is the second of five interlinking stories experimentally structured round the idea of a jazz composition, that will form Part One of the novel he is writing for his Ph.D. The rest are short stories, all written this year and thus expressing ideas and concerns that have been part of the individual learning process as the year has progressed, yet all speaking with engagingly original voices. Some thematic connections are discernible: Andrew Miller's *The Sweet and the Vile* uses the horrifying image of wife-as-corpse to look at the gap between the idealized world of advertised things and the quotidian experience of greedy, damaged humanity, and Judy Corbalis's *The Bridesmaid* expresses an adolescent's rage at discovering the true nature of the worlds intimate workings. Wilhelm Emilsson's *The Tuba Player* and Rinaldo Colombi's *These Hidden Gifts* show, I think, the continuing influence of the great South American post-modernists on the European imagination in their visions of disconnected eyes roaming a hospital room and a shower of tiny fish upon a railway station in Milan.

All the stories betray to some extent an agonized consciousness of the ruination of the world around us and engage with the struggles of the individual to impose an internal order upon an external chaos. In Philip McCann's *Grey Area* the narrator despairs in the end of any solution to disorder. These are new voices and we should listen. Paying attention to new writers should not merely be a game for publishers, for, in the words of Vaclav Havel, the writer has been blessed with the ability to articulate what is, in a manner of speaking, in the air; and, as we all know, what is in the air is a matter of life and death.

Rose Tremain
Norwich 1990

Rinaldo Colombi

This is a recent story by Rinaldo Colombi. He was
born in 1963 of Italian parents. While studying
Arts at Banbury, Leicester and Strasbourg, he held
a variety of jobs, including teaching English,
counselling youth offenders and factory work. He is
now working on his first novel in Norwich.

These Hidden Gifts

Through the gap between the carriage-ends I saw him. He stood out easily in his white jacket. Above the station the clouds were turning green and the brightness of midday had gone. He was shouting: 'Hot food. Lovely hot food.' I checked my watch. There was enough time before the train pulled out to make my way over for something to eat, so I picked up my small suitcase and started walking.

The wind swept warmly down the underpass from the platform entrances, bringing on it the smell of urine. There was more graffiti than when I last came to Milan, fibre-tipped signatures of travellers and a football fan's declaration in aerosol that: AC ARE FUCKERS. There were names everywhere and I was glad to come up level with the tracks to escape them.

At the sandwich bar I saw the food vendor more closely. He had black folds where his stubble fell in on itself. His face was dull from spending all day inside the station. His teeth were rounded, his hair oiled back over his scalp. I was drawn to his crafty eyes which were turned to the sky.

'Seems they're right with the forecast,' he said.

'Yes,' I replied.

'No doubt about it. Absolutely right. I just hope everyone heard the warning,' he said, still looking upwards.

'Just look at that sky. Did you ever see such a colour?'

He fixed his eyes on me.

'Travelling today, Signore?'

'Uhm,' I said vaguely, staring at the sweet cakes behind the glass.

'If you don't mind, may I ask where you are heading?'

'Venice,' I said, irritated that he was making conversation.

'That's a beautiful city,' he said. 'I'm very envious of you. I've been only twice, which is odd, you might think, considering how close it is to Milan. I'd like to travel more often, but my life is inside this station. Everyday I see people travelling, making journeys, going who knows where, and I stand behind this counter observing them.'

'Can you make me a sandwich,' I cut him short, looking at my watch.

'Certainly. What would you like?'

I hadn't thought about what I wanted even though the pastries were temptingly displayed in front of me.

'You know I play this sort of game,' he began, taking advantage of my indecision. 'I study people, how they're dressed, watching their expressions, the way they move, what bags they are carrying, who they are with, that sort of thing, and I try to establish their situation. I make a guess about where they're going and why.'

Rinaldo Colombi

'How ingenious,' I said drily, trying to think of a filling to choose that would take him the least amount of time to prepare. I looked at my watch, though I knew there was plenty of time before the train left.

He was impervious to my comment.

'Oh not really, Signore, its only a game I play and I'm probably wrong about most people. But because so many pass by I never get an opportunity to discover whether my guesses are correct.'

'I'm quite hungry,' I said. Could you fix me half a baguette with cheese and olives. And a cappuccino.

He nodded and, turning his back on me, began making the sandwich.

'Now, you for instance, Signore, check your watch repeatedly which suggests you are a time-conscious, and I would say, a punctual man.'

'Or simply apprehensive about the Venice train,' I said.

'Yes, it could be that,' he said cutting into the bread, 'but I don't think so. It's more likely a habit associated with your work. An office job or a transport official.'

The man's back was broad though slightly hunched at the shoulders. His oiled hair shone from the light reflected off his white jacket. It struck me that he was deluded by his own observations.

'Me, I don't wear a watch. I have no need for one. What with the clock in the station and announcements of arriving and departing trains, I always know the time.'

Slicing the cheese he said what he had committed to memory.

'You're dressed in casual clothes, Signore, so I think to myself, "He's on holiday." A small case – I'd say you've taken a week off work and are going to Venice for a break.'

He turned to look at me.

'Well, am I correct?'

'Astonishing. You're in the wrong job,' I said. He could not have been further from the truth about me.

He laughed. 'No disrespect, Signore, but you were one of the easier ones. It's your patience and mannerisms that give you away.'

'How's that sandwich coming along?' I asked.

'Be right with you. I'll get the coffee. The machine's good and hot at this time of day.'

He handed me the food and glanced up once more, the way he did when I first got close up to him.

'I can't fathom that sky for the life of me. Never seen such a thing.'

While he turned away to set the coffee running through the chromed Gaggia I looked again at the clouds bearing down on the station, at the strangeness of the colour. I resented him for having made apparent what had long since been so obvious to me.

As he ran the coffee he said, 'If you don't mind me asking, Signore, have you ever been married?'

'No,' I said.

'Close to it.'

'No,' I lied.

He frothed the milk with steam from the machine and poured it onto the coffee.

'Ah, perhaps you're fortunate. Mine was a failure. I married a younger woman, but she was too wild to settle down with me. Governed by routine, that's me, Signore.' And when he said it, he seemed genuinely sad. For the first time I felt like saying something honest to him, perhaps about why I was really going to Venice and whom I was meeting. But just then, when I wanted to be straight with him, I missed my opportunity. He gave me the cappuccino and a slip and said, 'Pay at the Cassa, Signore,' ending the conversation.

I paid the cashier with a 10,000 lire note, glad to be away from the food vendor but still thinking about the sadness in his voice.

I ate my sandwich near the bar, though far enough away to prevent conversation. I ate quickly, I wanted to get to the train. Behind I heard the vendor say, 'Seems they're right with the forecast.' Thinking he was addressing me, I turned only to realise he had repeated to another customer the words he first said to me. I hurried to finish my drink, returning the cup and saucer to the counter and, as was my custom, left a tip in a bowl of coins. The vendor thanked me. As I began to walk away he said something that stopped me dead.

'We all return to visit our pasts,' he said.

'What did you say?'

And he said it again, with total conviction, as if he knew exactly who was waiting for me in St Mark's Square. He said it with such timing and irony it was impossible to know one way or the other whether he had all that time been toying with me, playing on my insincerity, laughing to himself. He repeated, 'We all return to visit our pasts, Signore.'

I looked at his sharp eyes and the dark flesh beneath like two finger-swipes of soot, unable to move on. The vendor smiled at me, then peered up to the sky and said to the customer at the counter:

'I just hope everyone heard the warning.'

·

I must have missed the first flash of lightning when I was in the underpass, because as I came up the steps to the platform I flinched in surprise at the explosion of thunder. It began raining. The sky was by now an intense green and, walking towards the train, my head raised to the clouds, I overheard someone who spoke in a heavy country dialect saying how he'd never seen the sky turn such a colour and that in all his years in the fields he had never been so afraid of the weather. The rain became heavier and it had grown so dark in the station the long platform lights were switched on. They stuttered as a flash of lightning forked across the sky. I kept under the shelter but got drenched running across the platform and struggling with the door handle of the train.

I found a compartment and sat down opposite a man in a beautifully cut suit and a boy dressed in fine city clothes.

'Can you believe this rain?' he said.

'No,' I replied.

I removed my damp jacket and sat down. Opening my small case towards me and trying to avoid the man's face, I took out a paperback, placing it on the vacant seat beside me.

'You going all the way?' he inquired.

I nodded.

'I hope its finer over there,' he said.

'Lets hope so,' I said.

I clicked the suitcase shut and placed it on the rack above my head. The rain was drumming on the roof of the train.

'Every five seconds counts as a mile from the centre of the storm', the man told the boy. The boy's stare was made bigger by his tight collar. He sat stiffly in his expensive clothes listening to his father and I felt so certain that this boy would never have to want for anything during his childhood, I felt like cuffing him, just to spite the man's affluence.

There was another flash of lightning and the boy immediately counted aloud, telling the man, after a great tremor of thunder, they were two miles from the storm.

The man took down a newspaper and opened it precisely. Settling down I opened my book, but had hardly begun reading when the boy cried, 'Papa, look!'

'Sit nicely, Pino,' his father said, laying a hand on the boy's head without taking his eyes off the newspaper. 'Don't make a fool of yourself.'

But the boy fell over his lap, creasing the newspaper and said again, 'Look, Papa!'

The man rubbed the window and looked outside.

Further down the carriage there was a lot of noise and when I stood up to see what was happening I saw people crowding towards the windows. From the other end of the carriage I heard someone say, 'Its a miracle, I tell you.'

'Look out there,' the man said to me, and when I did I thought perhaps I was dreaming.

I hurried into the corridor and opened the door, stepping out into the rain. I bent down and picked up one of the tiny fish. It had blue markings on its back and it lay in my hand, like those paper fortune cut-outs from Christmas crackers that curl up in your palm. The rain poured down my face, then a shower of fish landed across my shoulders and I heard the sound of laughter. Someone placed a hand on my shoulder and, looking round, I saw a station guard wearing oil-skins.

'Better get inside, Signore,' he said. 'We're pulling out in a minute.'

I went into the toilet of the train and dried my hair with a towel. Then I returned to the compartment, got my suitcase and changed into dry clothes.

I looked at the station moving away from me. The lights were still on and those people waiting for other trains were huddled under the shelters. I saw the food vendor on the other side. He stood behind the counter, a startling figure in his white jacket. He was looking at me, I was sure of that. I was sure those dark eyes were staring at me as the train moved off.

At the end of the platform there was a group of boys in anoraks. They had plastic buckets by their feet and they were laughing excitedly. One wiped his hands down the thighs of his jeans and one on the seat of his pants. I just had time to glimpse another boy climbing down the iron frame of the roof support before the train took a bend. He jumped a last few feet onto the ground, dropping his bucket of shimmering fish which flapped in the puddles of rainwater for dear life.

Judy Corbalis

Judy Corbalis is a well-known children's writer. Born
and brought up in New Zealand, she taught in
secondary schools before coming to live in London
where she studied at LAMDA. She has worked in
television, fringe and community theatre. Since 1986
she has published five children's books. In 1988 she
adapted *The Snow Queen* for Theatre Foundry in
Birmingham and, in 1989, her book, *Oskar and the
Icepick* for BBC's Jackanory. She has also adapted her
children's stories for Thames Television.

The Bridesmaid

When I was ten and she was fourteen Jennifer Hartley-Burns was my idol and mentor. Everything she said and did was bathed in divine light. I admired the way she walked, hung on her every word and cherished as icons the postcards and letters she had sent me in the holidays and the programme from the school concert with her name next to mine. When she grew up Jennifer was going to either get married and have five children – three boys and twin girls – or be a nun. I was planning to get-married-and-live-happily-ever-after, having seen no other options bar the teachers at our school or the bag-lady who lived under Whetton Bridge in summer and in the doorway of Casey's Bottles o' Booze in winter. 'She turned down the prospect of a good sound man when she had one,' said Mumma, gleaming with self-righteousness. 'And look at her now!'

My brother Joseph and I were rather taken by the bag-lady's itinerant lifestyle but we had to agree that having no hot meals every night and no dear little children of your own seemed an unfortunate prospect. Neither of us thought to question who would be looking after the dear little children, or indeed, what constituted dear little children, which certainly couldn't have been us or anyone we knew. Nor whether the fact that the bag-lady would have been the one preparing, not receiving, the delicious hot meals, was what had driven her to baggery in the first place.

'A Tragic Waste,' said my mother, handing me a homemade Cornish pasty as I went off to meet Jennifer. 'Here, give her this on your way.' I hung from the top rail of the bridge. 'MILL-IE!' I called, leaning right over to see if I could spot her. I couldn't. I jumped up and down on the wooden slats. 'MILL-IE! I've brought you a homemade pasty!'

Millie appeared like a tortoise from under the shell of the bridge. She smiled at me and showed her worrying missing teeth. There was a rumour in my school that Millie was a witch and so cunning that she didn't switch personalities till dusk, the better to snare her victims. It was all rubbish, I knew, but I gazed anxiously at the sun to reassure myself that it was just a cloud passing over and it really was only four o'clock.

Millie took the pasty, smiling at me all the while. She poked the long end into her mouth, slobbered on it for a minute or two, then mashed it with her gums. She chewed with her whole cheeks and even her forehead working. I was compelled by revulsion to watch her eat the lot.

'She's disgusting!' I said excitedly, recounting it to Jennifer later.

'Poor thing,' said pious Jennifer. 'She doesn't know any better. You ought to be sorry for her, Mary.' Her halo grew before my worshipping gaze.

I was twelve before Jennifer decided to tell me about 'doing it'. She made me swear on the Bible not to pass the information on to a living soul, especially not to Joseph. This made sense. Joseph was only seven and a noted goody-goody who could not be trusted even with a bribe of threepence. I swore. 'You promise?' asked Jennifer solemnly. I nodded.

We were crouched under Whetton Bridge watching the turbulent muddy water bouncing over the rocks. It was spring, too early for Millie, and the thaw in the mountains twelve miles away had swollen the creek to three times its usual seasonal depth. This was causing me a lot of worry. The previous autumn my mother had knitted me a truly terrible cardigan in a colour she called oatmeal-flecked but which everyone in school knew as vomit-coloured. I'd put it on with a doomed heart and it had looked just as frightful as I had known it would.

'It's lovely,' I had lied politely, then, assuming a Jennifer expression, 'but it's much too nice for me. I'd like to be kind and give it to The Lepers.'

The Lepers were my mother's chosen charity. She had had a brief spell as a concerned community member driving the Handicapped School's bus but had been forced to retire ('I'm so sensitive All those poor little mongols distress me too much!') and had taken up Mr Tombley's Mission to Lepers instead.

So far, the Lepers had had my best woolly monkey, my Rupert Rabbit with the bent wire in his ear, two of my dolls, some special books and my brother's plush tiger and his kookabura mascot.

Joseph and I hated The Lepers. It served them right losing all their fingers and toes when they stole other people's things like that. We pored over the *Leper Man's* frequent brochures, torn between the secret thrill of the whole-bodied at the sight of the amputee and the outside hope that we might catch a glimpse of Rupert or Tiger in the background, peeping from a hut window or relaxing under a palm. Joseph, being younger, had spent several tearful nights distraught about Tiger's reaction to life in the leper colony.

'It's too hot for him,' he explained between sobs.

'He's used to the heat,' I said. 'Tigers come from hot countries.'

'He's missing me,' wept Joseph. 'He's never been away without me before. He doesn't know any lepers.'

'Let's look again,' I said, pulling open another concertinaed brochure. We scanned the pages.

HAPPY IN THE LOVE OF JESUS, MANUNU STILL CHEERFULLY

GATHERS COCONUTS USING HIS ELBOWS AND FEET, read the central page. No Tiger! We pored over the backdrops behind the earless leper playing the nose-flute and his friends washing the mission laundry with their stumps. There were a lot of coconuts but definitely no Tiger.

I had asked Jennifer what I could do. 'Tell him his tiger ran away,' she had said. 'It's very happy, living in a cave.'

'He'll ask me how I know.'

'Tell him you had a letter.'

'Yes, but he'll ask to see it.'

'Tell him Marilyn ate it before you could stop her.'

It had worked, too. Everyone knew Marilyn, our nanny goat, would eat anything she could reach. Joseph believed me completely. My regard for Jennifer had risen but my conscience was troubled. 'That was a lie. What I told Joseph,' I said.

'It was a good lie,' said Jennifer. 'Some lies are all right sometimes.'

'When?'

'When they make people feel better,' said Jennifer.

It seemed to me that all lies were told to make somebody feel better but I didn't want to challenge Jennifer's authority, so I didn't say so. 'Does God mind the good lies?'

'No,' said His spokeswoman unctuously. 'God understands.'

I began to wonder if God would consider the cardigan lie a kind and helpful one. Possibly. On the other hand, possibly not. Could I ask Jennifer? What if I did and she made me tell? She had done it before, the time David and I threw the mud balls at Mrs Benson's washing and the time I stole the chocolate fish from the sweet shop. Both times I had been smacked very hard but Jennifer had said at least my soul was clean and if I'd died in the night I'd have thanked her for being the one who'd made it possible for me to come face to face with Jesus without sin or stain. I wasn't very sure about coming face to face with Jesus. His hair looked a bit like Millie's. Loose and wild. But that was something else it might not be a good idea to say to Jennifer. If I told her about the cardigan and she refused to be my friend till I owned up, I'd have to tell. But if I didn't tell her . . .

'You're not listening,' said Jennifer irritably. I jerked to attention. The tumbling water scoured the banks, and the stones and soil where we crouched were damp and uncomfortable.

'I'm cold,' I complained.

'I think you're still too young to know about "doing it",' said Jennifer. 'Maybe I shouldn't tell you.'

'Yes. No, I'm not,' I said. 'I do want to hear. I really do.' I searched for a proper explanation for my inattention. 'I was just thinking about Jesus

27

actually.'

Jennifer began to giggle. 'You're AWFUL, Mary,' she said. 'Fancy thinking about *Jesus* doing that! No one would believe you're only twelve.' On the whole that seemed to be a compliment.

'I'm quite an advanced reader for my age,' I said.

I scanned the far bank as the cardigan crumbled into the swirling water. My mother had been deeply scathing that autumn about my offer to The Lepers. Not only did we not waste new things on lepers who, being natives, did not understand the difference between new and second-hand but what would someone in the tropics do with a heavy woollen garment? I had not thought of that. Defeated, I had slunk into my strait-jacket and set off for school.

And as I had been crossing the bridge, cursed and heavy-laden, salvation had descended on me. Unlike Saul, I had not gone blind, indeed my vision had seemed to clear to such an extent that the whole of the soft muddy autumn riverbank had refocused into a shimmering, beckoning vision. Twice before I had had these infant peak experiences when shining doorways had opened before me and showed me the true way forward. The first had been the time I had cut off beautiful baby Joseph's eyelashes with the bacon scissors, then jealously disposed of his shoulder-length ringlets. And the second had culminated when I bit right through Dr Weisenblum's hand as he approached to give me an injection. Whenever I thought about it, I could still taste the mixture of blood and satisfaction.

Since both these transcendental moments had been followed by retribution from either my mother or Dr Weisenblum, I had known what my ultimate fate would be. I had stood on the bridge wrestling. Long-term public humiliation or short-term private pain? The fools' gold in the rocks in the water had winked at me: the mud had had a faint golden glow. Did I want to be an occidental leper, mocked in the playground all winter? I had clambered over the end of the bridge and dropped onto the calling bank. Screened by the bridge from prying eyes, I had slipped off the vomit-bag, compressed it into a bundle and buried it deep in the clay.

But had I buried it deep enough? It had seemed like a huge hole in autumn but I had forgotten the vicious revealing waters of spring. Would I now be exposed for the liar and cheat I was? If my mother crossed Whetton Bridge might she look down and see below her, oozing from its grave, an arm of the beautiful oatmeal-flecked cardigan she had so lovingly knitted for me? What would it look like now? What happened to wool when you buried it?

For iniquity had paid off. I had told my mother someone at school had stolen the hideous thing and in a trembling voice had even suggested it might be some poor child who had no other warm winter garment. And she had believed me. Her belief was even more terrible to me than my own lie. To deceive your mother and SUCCEED? What kind of wicked child was I? Worse, how could I believe in her ever again? If I could lie to her so easily how could I have any faith in her at all? All winter, to test her, I had stolen from her purse. She had not noticed once and consequently, she had shrunk before my eyes and I hated her for not finding me out. But if she found out now it would be a disaster. Whatever God might think about necessary lies, Mumma certainly didn't approve of them.

Jennifer flung a stone at the other bank. 'You're too young,' she said again.

'You just said I was old for twelve,' I said indignantly.

'Yes, but not old like that,' she said.

I could see she was losing interest in being with me. 'All right,' I said. 'Don't tell me then. Just don't expect me to be your bridesmaid, that's all.'

The bridesmaid fantasy was an old one and very well-known in my family. The first time Jennifer had mentioned it I was only nine, had thought she'd meant she was marrying right away and had gone home demanding an instant outfit. It had taken several phone calls to Jennifer's family to convince me I was wrong. In the ensuing three years, while Jennifer and I made wedding plans, I had been clothed variously in pale blue satin, an English Liberty flowered smock, an apple-green silk dress with a pink sash ('Apple tree and apple blossom,' Jennifer had explained) and in pure white, like the bride, but with a Hartley-Burns tartan sash. 'A strangely little-known clan, the Hartley-Burns,' remarked my father. 'I expect old Cedric's the *Burn* of MacBurns if only we knew.'

My grandmother, who was staying with us again, told him to stop being unkind. 'Not unkind,' said my father. 'Realistic.'

'What's realism got to do with it?' said my grandmother. 'It's hardly Cedric's fault, after all.'

I knew Cedric was Jennifer's father. 'What's not Cedric's fault?' I asked. My grandmother looked at my father. 'Pas devant,' she said. 'I told you.'

'Not before what?' I said.

'Christ,' said my father. 'They teach her French at that school? I thought it was all fashion and weddings.'

My grandmother turned on him sharply. 'I wish you'd stop it,' she said. 'We all know what's the matter with you. And if you go on seeing her, you know just what the outcome will be. Really, a married man your age ought to have more sense.'

She looked at me. 'Go and do your homework, Mary.'

'I've done it already,' I said.

'As a matter of interest,' said my father, 'who's the bridegroom?'

'What bridegroom, Dada?'

'Jennifer's. I assume if she's getting married there is a husband. Or is she having a solo wedding?'

'I don't know,' I said. The idea of the bridegroom didn't really interest me. After all, he wouldn't be wearing a proper bridal outfit like me and Jennifer.

'Leave her alone,' said my grandmother. 'Go and find something to do, Mary.'

'What?' I said.

My father raised his eyes. 'Skipping?'

'It's raining, Dada.'

'Don't you start,' warned my grandmother, and to me she said, 'What would you like to do?'

I seized my chance. 'Please may I look at the Journal?'

It was the 'may' that did it. Even my father was impressed.

'Well, all right,' she said. 'But be very, very careful.'

'Promise, Ga,' I said, and I slipped off to get it before she could change her mind.

The Journal belonged to Ga because it had been her father's. He'd been away a lot when Ga was growing up so she hadn't known him very well but he'd left her the Journal when he died. It was a diary of his life when he was a war correspondent with the army fighting in the desert, Ga said. As well as what he'd written, there were a lot of photographs of Ga and Uncle Charles and Uncle Edward and Uncle Cecil and poor Mama who died when Ga was thirteen. But best of all were the drawings. Palm trees, crocodiles, mud houses, camels, women in a boat on a river, some pyramids, pots and vases, a man in a dress, men going into a cave – the Journal had dozens of tiny pictures drawn all the way through. I particularly liked the one of the crocodile eating the little boy.

I had a special system for looking at the Journal. I took it out of its silk cloth, laid it down carefully, then, closing my eyes, let it fall open at random. If it opened at the crocodile, it was a very good omen. That day, however, its stiff dust-smelling pages split apart at a whole page of writing and a photograph. The writing was in copper-plate and I could read it without too much difficulty but I was disappointed at the lack of a drawing. I thought about turning over but it would have been cheating. I looked at the photograph.

Nearly a century away, my great-grandfather sat with his elbow on his desk, his face shaded from the Empire sun by a solar topee. He contemplated his latest dispatches untroubled by the waterfall pouring from the left corner of the photograph to form a river in front of his desk. I knew this was how it must have been all along the Nile. Little desks set up by natives in the mud beside the cooling water. The gun propped by his chair would be for protection from the crocodiles. I had frequently heard the story of the Brave Little Egyptian Girl whom my great-grandfather had personally seen save her baby brother from a crocodile's jaws by pushing her thumbs into the wicked beast's eyes and blinding it, so I understood the dangers of the riverbank. I had always had a secret worry that I should be unable to perform such a noble act if called upon to rescue Joseph and whenever we went on family picnics, I checked the banks for long stretches on either side of our site. My family had little sympathy with these precautions and my father constantly directed me back to the passage in the encyclopaedia which said that crocodiles did not live in temperate countries.

But I had secret knowledge of my own. What was a taniwha but a crocodile in disguise?

'There aren't any taniwhas,' said my father wearily.

'There could be. There might be one left over.'

'Not in this river.'

'But, Dada, what if there is?'

We repeated this at every picnic and at that point he would sigh or curse and leave me to get on with Crocodile Patrol.

I finished examining the photograph and began poring over the writing. Dada and Ga were arguing quite loudly. I could hear them even from that distance. 'She won't be back till you make a decision and stick by it,' said Ga.

'It's none of your business,' said Dada. I could tell he was starting to lose his temper. 'Stop interfering.'

'Interfering!' said Ga. 'I see. I should just let you get on with wrecking four people's lives and stay at home and say nothing.'

'If you didn't come rushing down as soon as she asked you, I might have been able to talk her round.'

'That's exactly why she asked me, I expect,' said Ga in a steely tone. 'Perhaps you'd better go away and think about it. I'm certainly not looking after your washing or cooking. I'm disgusted by the way you're going on. Like a boy of fourteen.'

I heard a door slam, then silence. I went back to the copperplate, half-listening to Ga taking bowls out of cupboards, flour out of drawers, thumping spoons, clacking the sifter. I went on reading till the air felt a bit quieter, then I went back into the kitchen.

Ga was rolling out scone dough. Cheese, not raisin. I could see the yellow worms in it. 'What's pro-cliv-eyety?' I asked.

'Proclivity. Whose?'

'Lord Kitchener's unfortunate.'

She took the kitchen knife and slashed the dough into nine large squares. 'A bad habit Lord Kitchener had.'

'Why was it unfortunate?'

'He probably wasted too much time on it. Like you with your questions.'

'Yes, but what was it?'

'I told you. A bad habit. He was rude to the natives sometimes.'

'The Maoris?'

'No. The Sudanese. In Africa. Just below the pyramids.'

'Were they cross about it?'

'Who?'

'The Sudanese.'

'More uncomfortable, I should think.' She pulled out the oven tray and lifted the scones onto it in one whole block. 'Did you put the Journal away properly?'

'Yes.'

'Good girl. Now go out to the greenhouse and look at the guava tree. There's one on it nearly ripe. If it smells ready, you can have it. Only if it's ready, mind.'

This was a great honour. Joseph would be really jealous. I raced outside and sniffed at the pale pink fruit, hoping to catch the lemony pear-tomato smell that showed it was ripe. It wasn't. I trailed back inside.

'It's not.'

My grandmother was lying upside-down on the ironing board which she'd wedged in a diagonal between the sink and the Kelvinator. She was in her Gayelord Hauser phase right then which meant she ate a lot of yoghurt and spinach and lay upside down on the ironing board at intervals every day chanting things like, *Every day in every way, I grow stronger and stronger.* Or, *Whatever happens is for the best in the best of all possible worlds.* It drove Dada crazy. 'Better than the Theosophists,' said Mumma.

'Christ,' said Dada, 'why can't I have normal relations like everybody else?'

Ga's eyes were shut. '*Beauty is Truth, Truth Beauty,*' she intoned. '*That is all ye know on Earth and all ye need to know.* I'm sorry, Mary. It looked as if it would be ready by today.'

'And I'm all wet,' I said accusingly.

Ga sat up on the ironing board and slung her legs onto the floor. 'I'll make a cup of tea,' she said. 'Just for you and me. And we'll have the best scones.'

'Can I have the guava tomorrow?'

'It's yours,' said Ga. She edged round the board to fill the kettle. I watched her. I loved Mumma, of course but Ga was special. She wasn't like other people's grandmothers. Jennifer didn't even have any grandparents because her mother and father were old but Ga was so young that everyone thought she was our mother, not Mumma's. She smoked and wore slacks in the winter and a green bikini in summer. Not one single other person on the whole beach had a bikini. Sometimes she and I took baths together. Ga's bosoms were little and crumpled up. 'Very fashionable,' said Ga. 'And very twenties. Not like those ugly great melons some women have. I was a beauty in the twenties, you know.' Ga had two boyfriends, Lance, an American who gave me chewing-gum, and Douglas who took us out in his boat. Joseph and I had automatically assumed that anyone who came courting Ga was obliged to make good with us. Lance had given Ga a black satin nightie. After our joint bath I was usually al-lowed to rub Ga's Elizabeth Arden Orange Skin Food into my face and neck, dab myself with her Arpège perfume (Douglas), climb into the satin nightie and spend the night in the spare double bed with her.

I watched her fondly as she buttered our scones. 'Can I sleep in your bed to-night?'

'I suppose so,' said Ga. 'But you'll have to try not to kick.' She passed me my tea and sat down with hers. 'How's Jennifer?' she said.

'She's all right,' I said. 'It's her birthday next week. I'm going to buy her a present in Woolworths.'

'That's nice,' said Ga. 'How old will she be this time?'

'Sixteen.'

'Mmmn,' said Ga. 'Are you missing Mumma?'

'No,' I said. 'It's better with you. But Joseph is.'

'Joseph's younger. Why is it better with me?'

I considered. 'Well, there's the nightie. And sleeping in your bed. And you don't make us be generous to the lepers.'

My grandmother sighed. 'Watch out for the good people in this world,' she said. 'They're the ones who create all the problems for the rest of us.'

'I thought it was the poor,' I said. 'That's what they say at Sunday School. And the evil.'

'Oh, the evil,' said Ga. 'Well, at least they're enjoying themselves. It's the improvers that cause all the trouble. Don't turn into an improver, whatever you do.'

'Will I?'

'I doubt it,' said Ga. 'It usually skips a generation. Is Jennifer having a party?'

'No.'

'Just some friends around?'

'No, only me,' I said proudly. 'I'm her best friend. We're going to the Sing-ing Kettle for tea.'

Ga revolved her cup. 'Doesn't she have any friends her own age?'

Judy Corbalis

'No,' I said. 'She likes me best. And I'm old for nearly twelve. Everyone says so.'

'Yes,' said Ga. 'I know. But that's not the point. She ought to have some friends nearer her age. An eleven-year-old's too young for a sixteen-year-old.'

'Nearly twelve,' I repeated, hurt. 'And we've been best friends for ages.'

'Have you ever been to her house?'

'No, but she's come here lots of times. And I'm going to be her bridesmaid when she gets married.'

'I know,' said Ga, 'I know all about that. Here, take this scone to Joseph. He's in the shed.'

'Can I take one for Marilyn?'

'Marilyn doesn't know the difference between a scone and a tin can,' said Ga. 'If you want to feed Marilyn, take the scraps bucket with you out of the washhouse on your way. And mind she doesn't eat your raincoat.'

I bought Jennifer a china donkey pulling a china cart full of china flowers, and a box of Winning Post chocolates. It took all my pocket-money but she was so pleased, especially with the chocolates, it was worth it. 'I've never had a whole box all to myself before,' she said. We were having tea and fairy cakes in the Singing Kettle.

'Joseph and I always get one at Christmas. From Ga. But they're all mint ones.'

'A box each?'

'Yes.'

She was impressed. 'I like your grandmother,' she said. 'But my mother thinks she shouldn't have boyfriends like that.'

I was torn between embarrassment that Ga should have offended Jennifer's mother and an urge to defend her. 'They're not really boyfriends,' I explained. 'They're just her unfortunate proclivity.'

Jennifer seemed satisfied by this. 'Well, that's different,' she said. She smiled at me. 'I've got a surprise.'

'For your birthday?'

'No. Not till next weekend. Because you're my best friend, Mother says I can ask you to stay.'

'At your house?'

'Yes. She'll pick you up on Friday and we can go to school on Monday together.'

I was ecstatic. A weekend at the house of my best friend!

'Will your mother let you come?'

'I'm always allowed to stay with people,' I said. 'That's wonderful!'

I had never been inside Jennifer's house. The Hartley-Burns lived a long way from us on the outskirts of town in one of the few two-storey houses I had ever seen. They had a tennis court at the front and a glasshouse at the side of the garden.

'Will we sleep upstairs?'

'Yes,' said Jennifer. 'In my room. Beatrix says she doesn't mind moving out.' Beatrix was her elder sister whom I'd met once or twice when the Hartley-Burns had come to collect or deposit Jennifer at our house. 'Bring your racquet,' she said. 'It's a bit late but we can still play if it doesn't rain.' I winged my way home to break the news. 'Guess what? I'm going to stay a whole weekend with Jennifer! Her mother said.'

Ga was still staying with us but Mumma was back home. 'I don't know about that, Mary,' she said.

I was taken aback. 'Mumma! Why not?'

'It's too much work for Jennifer's mother,' she said.

'But she asked me!'

'I don't think it's a good idea,' she said.

I was furious. 'She's my best friend! Why can't I go? You just want to spoil it for me. You're mean and nasty.'

'Mary!' said my mother warningly.

'Well, it's true. You are. You don't want me to have a good time. You're jealous just because she's my best friend.' My cheeks were hot with rage and frustration. 'You can't stop me. I'll pack my bags and go even if you don't let me. And if you don't watch out, I might stay there for good.'

'Then I'll be an only child,' said Joseph who'd been watching the scene with enjoyment.

'Goody goody,' I sneered.

'Mary's being mean,' he wailed.

Ga's voice came booming out of the carpet. 'For Heaven's sake, be quiet both of you!' She was doing yoga and had to stand on her head or shoulders four times a day for her blood. She had her legs propped against the wall by the tea towel from bonnie Scotland and her slacks were all rucked up round her calves. Her voice sounded deeper upside-down.

'Why can't she go, Eleanor?'

'You know perfectly well why not.'

'I don't see that she'll come to any harm.'

'Jennifer's my friend,' I squawked. 'She likes me.'

'Be quiet, Mary!' snapped Ga. I shut up. 'She's got to find out sooner or later.'

'She's only eleven, Mother. Don't be ridiculous.'

'She's almost twelve, actually, and at twelve I delivered poor Mama's last baby when the doctor's trap overturned and he couldn't get there in time.'

'That was over forty years ago, Mother. Things are different now.'

'Not so different,' said Ga. 'I should let her go, Eleanor. She's a sensible child. She can cope.'

'I am sensible,' I broke in, 'Miss Carter said so today in class. And anyway, I don't know why you're all going on as if there's something wrong with going to Jennifer's. I thought you'd be pleased.' And I burst into tears.

'We are pleased,' said Ga. 'Aren't we, Eleanor? You go and have a good time. Your mother's got one or two things on her mind right now.'

I sniffed loudly. 'Can I use your Orange Skin Food?'

'Only a dab,' said Ga. 'I'm nearly out of it.'

The weekend after that I went to stay with Jennifer. I took my racquet and overnight case to school and Mrs Hartley-Burns picked us up in the Morris Minor. 'Jump in, girls,' she cried brightly. 'Super to see you, Mary.' We clambered in and squashed together in the back seat. As we swung in at their front gate, my blur of excitement was tinged with awe. A two-storey house. With stairs. An upstairs bedroom. I had only ever lived in a single-storey house and the idea of a second floor above my head seemed romantic beyond dreams. I stood in the hall clutching my case and staring. A wooden staircase curved elegantly up and round to a landing above me. 'Show Mary up, Jen,' said her mother. We took my case and racquet and started the magic climb.

Jennifer's bedroom was the third room along. From behind the second door, which was closed, came loud snores. 'Daddy,' explained Jennifer. 'He gets tired easily.' She pushed her own door wide open. 'There,' she said expansively. I don't remember what I was expecting but I can still recall my acute disappointment at the sight of the two iron bedsteads covered with white candlewick bedcovers, the white chest of drawers and the ugly big wooden wardrobe. The curtains were striped and skimpy, there was a small rag rug on the floor. 'It's lovely,' I said, wanting to cry.

'I knew you'd like it,' said Jennifer. The snoring was coming through the wall. Jennifer rapped sharply on the plaster. 'Stop it, Daddy!' The snoring diminished. 'I'll show you the bathroom,' Jennifer said. 'Then we'll have supper.'

I can't remember much about the supper either but I had trouble swallowing owing to the lump in my throat. Somehow I had envisaged Jennifer in a completely different environment. I thought of Ga and a warm bath and the Orange Skin Food.

'Do you use Orange Skin Food?' I asked Mrs Hartley-Burns to be polite.

'Cosmetics are an unnatural affront to the Lord, Mary,' said Mrs Hartley-Burns. 'If God had meant us to have red lips, we'd have been born with them.'

Derek, Jennifer's brother, who came between her and Beatrix in age, looked at me. 'D'you play tennis?' he asked.

'I brought my racquet,' I said miserably.

'Good,' he said. 'It's going to be fine tomorrow. We can make up a four.'

Daddy was not at supper. 'Too tired, I'm afraid,' said Jennifer's mother. 'He'll catch up with you in the morning.' We played dominoes and consequences and Pelmanism round the kitchen table until it was time for bed.

The kitchen had seemed rather cold to me but the hall was icy. As we went upstairs, I leaned over the banisters and looked down at the chequer-board pattern of the hall floor. After all, I was going to be sleeping upstairs. That was something to have over Joseph. I began to cheer up and by the time Jennifer and I had changed and climbed between our frozen white sheets, I was feeling much better. We spent a long time giggling and talking in the dark. We completely altered my bridesmaid's outfit to peach satin with ecru crochet trim and dyed matching satin shoes.

'My grandmother's got a satin nightie,' I offered.

'Really?'

'Yes.'

'What colour?'

'Black. And I wear it sometimes.' Jennifer gave a sigh. Envy of luxury was inherent in it. 'You can try it on one day if you like.'

'Oh yes,' she said. 'Please. You are lucky, Mary.'

Jennifer's own pyjamas were thick men's ones. Her mother had been worried that my winceyette nightdress with pink floral rosebuds would not be warm enough but I'd reassured her. If I was cold in bed I would get out and put my jersey on. We talked and giggled and made plans as the beds slowly warmed up a few degrees, then finally we fell asleep.

I woke up to the disorientation of a strange bedroom. Jennifer was awake already and as I climbed out into the sharp-edged early autumn cold, she said, 'Make sure you put your jersey on. It's cold in the drawing-room.' The drawing-room! I was again transported to another world. Did the Hartley-Burns have breakfast in a drawing-room? The grandeur of it was overwhelming. My clothes felt damp and clammy and I had goosebumps on my arms. We went off and cleaned our teeth and washed our faces, then I followed Jennifer down the staircase and up to the double doors I'd noticed on the way in last night. She pushed them apart. A freezing wave of air came swelling out and I shivered. There was no heating at all in the drawing-room. The fireplace was ghostly empty, its grate bars forlornly waiting to be stacked and heaped. On the slate hearth to the left of its fireless yawn was an enamel jug full of rosehips swaying dismally in the chimney's cold breath. At the side of the fireplace stood an old leather chair with buttons on its back, and, opposite that, a large battered floral sofa. In the bay window was a pretty desk I knew Mumma would like and there was a half-circle table against the far wall. Jennifer knelt down on the rug in front of the fireplace, her back to the grate. 'Just kneel by me,' she whispered. I moved to the side where the draught felt less cold and sank down next to her. I then realised that Beatrix was already kneeling in the bay window by the desk where a few beams of early April sun were filtering in. What was I supposed to do now?

Derek came sullenly in, arguing about something with his mother who appeared behind him, bright and eager.

'Good morning, girls,' she said. 'I hope you slept well, Mary.'

'Yes, thank you,' I replied, still baffled by the breakfast arrangements. At my house we had it at an ordinary kitchen table. 'Just waiting for Daddy,' said Mrs Hartley-Burns. She put her head round the door. 'Daddy!' There was a noise I couldn't identify, Mrs Hartley-Burns sank to her knees, the door opened again and Daddy came in.

I had never met Jennifer's father. It was always her mother who dropped her and collected her but that was normal enough. Most of the mothers did that. I had never even thought very much about the fact that she had a father. I assumed all fathers were much like my own. So I was not prepared for Daddy. He was very, very old with a blank baby's face and wispy grey hair at the sides of his head. He rocked as he walked and his head kept slipping sideways. There was drool bubbling at the side of his mouth. I thought of Millie and the pasty.

'This is Mary, Daddy,' said Mrs Hartley-Burns. 'Jennifer's friend.' Daddy looked at me with benign vacuity. 'He's absolutely thrilled to meet you at last,' said Mrs Hartley-Burns. 'Aren't you, Daddy? He's heard so much about you.'

'How do you do?' I said. 'I'm going to be Jennifer's bridesmaid.'

'Isn't that super?' said his wife.

Daddy looked at me from large empty dilated pupils. He was smiling into the far distance. 'Come over here, Daddy,' said Mrs Hartley-Burns. 'By me.'

Daddy moved towards her. As he walked he drifted from foot to foot and glided and swayed like a man underwater, aimlessly heading for an unknown goal. His wife caught him by the wrist and swung him towards her. He knelt down. 'Very good, Daddy,' said Beatrix and Jennifer encouragingly. I stole a look at everybody. Jennifer didn't seem to see anything odd about Daddy's behaviour and nor did Beatrix. Derek, however, looked sullen and embarrassed. Their mother was clearly preparing for something: she had a blue book open in front of her and an enthusiastic look on her face. 'Close your eyes!' she said in a singing voice. 'And let us pray! Oh, Jesus, who sees our every sin and every blemish, open our eyes to Thine ever-loving kindness. Make clean our hearts within us and mercifully hear us when we call upon Thee.'

'Amen,' said Derek, Beatrix and Jennifer. Jennifer nudged me. I opened my eyes. Mrs Hartley-Burns was looking at me with her eyebrow raised. 'Amen,' I croaked. She smiled.

'Oh, Jesus, Light of the World and Salvation of the Life to come, hear these Thy servants, Albinia, Cedric, Beatrix, Derek and Jennifer and our guest, Mary Fredrickson, as they call upon Thee to cleanse them from all sin and stain.'

My stomach rumbled loudly. Derek grinned at me. 'Imbue Thy servants with righteousness,' implored Mrs Hartley-Burns. 'And make Thy chosen people joyful.'

'Amen,' cried everyone, me included.

Mrs Hartley-Burns continued with a request for peace in the world, a lot of promises to Jesus to behave well and a wish for eternal life. She concluded that we all wanted to be made better people through Jesus and to become servants and missionaries of God. Mr Tombley was a missionary of God, I knew. I prayed silently and explained to God that it was all a mistake and that I did not ever want to be a missionary.

'We will now have an inward prayer,' said Mrs Hartley-Burns. 'Just ask God to grant you any little thing in your heart. But don't be greedy, please. God loveth not the greedy man.' I asked God for a new jar of Orange Skin Food for Ga. If it came soon, Ga would give me the old jar with the remains of the cream. 'And now for the hymn,' she said. *All Things Bright and Beautiful .'*

I knew it without the book but I felt really stupid singing it with just the six of us. Daddy didn't sing but made low crooning noises and smiled a lot.

Following their mother's lead, Beatrix, Derek and Jennifer got to their feet, Daddy and I close behind, and filed into the kitchen for breakfast. Daddy sat at the head of the table as Mrs Hartley-Burns took the bacon and eggs out of the Aga and set them down in front of us. 'Daddy's had his already,' she said. He sat smiling and drooling,

Watching us all eating. I chewed on my bacon and egg and tried not to stare at him. If I thought too much about the drooling, my stomach would start lurching and my throat would gag. I concentrated hard on the weather. The kitchen was wonderfully warm after the drawing-room. Derek and Beatrix were arguing about whether it would be too cold for tennis.

'It's a hard court,' said Derek. 'And the sun's out now.'

After we'd done the washing-up I went upstairs, got my racquet and went out to the court. Derek had said a foursome, so I was surprised to see his parents by the court with their racquets too. 'We'll all play,' said Beatrix. 'Mother and Daddy and I'll be at this end and Derek and Jennifer and Mary at the other.' I'd never played in a sixsome before though I was good at tennis and went to a Saturday club in the season. 'You stand forward, Derek,' said Jennifer, 'and we'll go by the line.' We tossed a coin for service and Beatrix's end won. She served to me and I returned it. The ball fell gently next to Daddy's racquet.

'Come on, Daddy,' roared the Hartley-Burnses encouragingly. Daddy looked dazed, raised his racquet, batted it feebly at the air and smiled at us.

'Jolly good, Daddy!' called Mrs Hartley-Burns, swooping in behind him and returning the ball which had bounced twice. 'Nearly got it that time.' Even Joseph would have seen that was a lie. I was so engrossed in watching Daddy, I missed my own return shot. 'Hard luck, Mary!' cried Mrs Hartley-Burns.

It suddenly dawned on me that I was participating in a real-life school story. The people were not quite right but the language was clearly recognizable to anyone who had swallowed my diet of Brazil and Blyton. All my life I had longed to have a midnight feast in the dorm, to play lacrosse and eat tuck, and, unexpectedly, my wish had been granted. I had been precipitated into the school holiday version of my dream. Over the course of the game, I became so carried away by this idea that I found myself quite naturally shouting 'Tophole!' when Derek hit a decisive ace.

'Game!' said Beatrix.

'Don't forget a little rally for Daddy,' said Mrs Hartley-Burns starting to go inside. Was he her Daddy? I didn't like to be rude and ask.

'My father used to be a provincial tennis champion,' I told her as she went by. 'That's why I get coaching.'

'Terrific,' she said. 'Super. So just have a little to-and-fro with Daddy before I come and take him in.'

Daddy began to giggle. He put down his racquet and clapped his hands. Beatrix threw the ball to him and he shambled after it and clumsily picked it up. 'Come on,' said Jennifer. 'Let's go in and see what there is for lunch.'

Now I understood the nature of where I was, things slotted happily into place. Not even morning prayers seemed bizarre in that context. Even Daddy seemed somehow correct. I floated happily through the rest of the visit, murmuring appropriate responses from time to time and returned ecstatic to my family after school on Monday.

'Did you enjoy it?' asked my father.

'Super,' I said. 'Tophole, actually.' He groaned. 'Daddy's funny, though. But he likes me. Everybody noticed.'

'You see,' said Ga to Mumma. 'I told you.'

'Ga,' I said. 'Whose father is he?'

'Jennifer's, of course,' said Mumma.

'Why's he like that?'

'He was mustard-gassed in the First World War,' said Ga. 'He used to be quite normal before.'

'Heaven knows why Albinia married him,' said my mother.

'Some people,' said Dada, 'think he got the raw end of the deal. Did you have morning prayers, Mary?'

'Oh yes,' I said, 'and evening too on Sunday. And we changed my bridesmaid's dress. It's going to be pale peach satin with . . .'

'Somebody stop her,' said Dada. 'I can't stand it.'

'There's a boy in my school,' said Joseph, competing, 'who can whistle through his tummy button.'

'Navel,' said Ga who liked us to give things anatomical their proper names.

'Navel, then. He can whistle, *Oh I Do Like to be Beside the Seaside* . He's going to teach me.'

Our father got up from the table. 'Excuse me from the pudding,' he said. 'It's excitement. A professional bridesmaid and a navel virtuoso in the same family. It's too much glory for one householder to contain.' He went out.

Ga looked at Mumma. 'I know where he's going,' said Mumma miserably, 'but what can I do about it?'

'Out you two,' said Ga. 'Right now. Off and play and don't come back till I call you.' We went.

Joseph was seven. He still believed in ghosts and the tooth fairy. 'Let's feed Marilyn,' he said, picking up some windfalls from under the apple tree.

'I'll tell you about Jennifer's house,' I said.

'I don't want to hear about her house,' said Joseph. 'Why was Mumma crying?'

'She wasn't, you big baby,' I said, even though I knew she had been.

As I sat under the bridge with Jennifer, I couldn't stop thinking about Mumma's crying and about how she didn't notice when I stole from her purse and how Lance had brought Joseph a wind-up car and only a silly baby doll for me and how often Dada wasn't at home and how I'd had to stop having baths with Ga because I didn't want her to see I'd started growing big ugly melon breasts. I felt overwhelmed with misery.

'Just don't expect me to be your bridesmaid, that's all,' I said nastily.

'Of course you will,' said Jennifer. 'You can be chief bridesmaid if you want.' She lowered her voice. 'When you're married you'll have to do it, you know,' she whispered.

'I will not,' I said.

'You know what happens?' she asked.

'Ga told me,' I said.

'Have you seen Joseph's thing?'

'Of course I have.'

'When?'

'In the bath,' I said. 'Only I have baths by myself now.'

Judy Corbalis

'Beatrix and I've never bathed with Derek,' Jennifer said. 'But I saw his thing once when he was getting changed after tennis.' She snickered. 'That's what they use,' she said. 'That's how you get a baby.' Her face looked greedy and secret.

'I know that,' I said. 'Ga told me. And it isn't a thing. It's a penis.'

'MARY!' Jennifer was shocked. 'That's filthy! Fancy saying it out loud.'

'It is called that,' I said irritably. 'I saw it in *The Book of the Human Body*. Ga showed me.'

'Your grandmother must be disgusting, showing you that.'

'I thought you were going to tell me about "doing it",' I said. 'I know all that already.'

'Yes, but do you know what they actually do?'

I thought back to what Ga had said. 'The man's got a penis and the woman's got a space,' I said. I couldn't remember the name of the space. 'And he puts his penis against her space and drops a seed in and then she gets a baby.'

I had a mental picture of a man in his suit, gabardine raincoat and hat, politely raising the hat as he pressed himself against the woman. She was wearing a print floral dress which she'd kindly lifted up to allow him to perform the clinical, perfunctory action which would yield them the baby they wanted now they were married. Jennifer looked at me triumphantly. 'I knew you didn't know! He doesn't just put it against her, stupid, he pokes it right inside her.'

It was the first time she had ever called me stupid. I looked at her, dazed and hurt. 'He does not!'

'Yes, he does,' she said, exultant. 'And what's more YOUR OWN MOTHER AND FATHER have done it. Twice, at least. They must have. They've got you and Joseph.'

I was absolutely disgusted. 'You're wrong,' I said loudly. 'It's not true.'

'Right inside her,' said Jennifer. 'And it is true. And you'll have to do it one day too.'

Somewhere deep down in myself I knew she was right. There had always been a secret that I hadn't known about, that Joseph didn't know about, that everyone in my class at school didn't know about, even though we all knew vaguely and namelessly that it existed.

'You're a filthy, wicked liar, Jennifer Hartley-Burns!' I shouted. 'And I'm going to tell on you.' I knew I sounded like Joseph but I couldn't help it. 'I hate you! And I'm never going to be your bridesmaid, ever!' I cast about for some way to hurt her back. A movement at the top of the bank caught my eye. A shambling wild-haired figure laden with bags was picking her way down the bank to her spring and summer home under the bridge. She drooled and smiled to herself as she concentrated all her attention on keeping her bags clear of the damp soil. 'Well, your parents didn't do it,' I said spitefully. 'They couldn't

42

have, could they? Not with your father like that.' I saw by her face that I had hit my target. 'He can't even pick up a tennis ball properly. He probably hasn't even got a penis.' Her face crumpled. 'Millie ought to be your mother,' I said. 'She'd be exactly right for your father. Two mental people doing it. You ought to bring him to live under Whetton Bridge with her. They could slobber away together.'

I couldn't believe I was really saying it. I felt shocked and excited and cruel. Jennifer burst into tears. Power scoured the banks of my remaining decency and they crumbled. 'You'd better never have any children,' I said. 'They'll probably turn out like your father.' I tapped the side of my forehead with my forefinger. Jennifer just sat there with tears running down her face. She looked awful. I couldn't see why I'd ever liked her. I got up and clambered up the bank, sticking out my tongue at Millie as I passed her.

I went straight home, my chest gripped with power and hate and grief. Joseph was playing in the yard. He had scraped out roads in the soil for his matchbox cars and was contentedly driving them round and round. I scuffed out some of the roads with my foot. 'Don't, Mary,' he said, re-making them.

'You listen to me, Joseph Fredrickson,' I said. 'There's no tooth fairy and no Father Christmas, either.' Joseph looked at me, startled. 'There *is* so a tooth fairy,' he said. 'She gave me sixpence for my double tooth.'

'You're just dumb,' I said. 'Fancy believing that. It's not the tooth fairy, it's Mumma and Dada. And at Christmas, too. Father Christmas is for babies, Stupid.' He gave me a stricken look. 'And another thing,' I said. 'About Tiger. He's dead. He caught leper's disease and his legs and tail fell off and he starved to death. And that's the truth.' Joseph opened his mouth and began to scream. Ga would be out any moment now to see what the matter was. 'And I'll tell you what else,' I said. 'You're adopted. You don't really belong to us. Nobody round here wants you. They're sending you back to your real parents soon. Mumma told me.' The awful sobs and screams followed me as I stalked off inside to my bedroom.

I took my Chinese box off my dressing-table. It was red with a gold dragon on it. Jennifer had given it to me: it was my most treasured possession. Inside it were all her letters and postcards and a real gold locket with a picture of Ga as a baby. I opened the box, took out the locket, then shut the box again and went back outside with it. I could hear Joseph sobbing in the kitchen. The sound followed me all the way down the garden, right to the back.

Marilyn looked up as I approached. Her eyes were like the devil's and she had bad breath. She waggled her beard and bleated. I held out the box to her. 'Here you are, Marilyn,' I said. She seized the red lacquered end and began to crunch on it. For a split second I tried to pull it away but Marilyn jerked her head sideways wrenching it out of my fingers. I watched dry-eyed as she chewed up my box, my letters and my postcards, then I went back up to the house.

I felt so old I could hardly bear it. I veered away at the back door: I couldn't face what was going to happen inside. Instead, I went back to Whetton Bridge. And underneath it, with Millie incuriously laying out her belongings and setting up her spring and summer house opposite me, I sat and wept and wept for my red Chinese box and the buried cardigan and Tiger and the tooth fairy and Joseph and Jennifer and my big new melon breasts and because I could tell lies to Mumma and not be found out and, most of all, for Crocodile Patrol which I knew I would never need to do again since I finally understood that crocodiles don't ever live in temperate countries.

Wilhelm Emilsson

Wilhelm Emilsson was born in 1965 in Reykjavik
where he studied for his degree. His work first
appeared in a collection featuring winners of the
1986 Icelandic Arts Festival Short Story
Competition. Since then he has been published
in various magazines

The Tuba Player

The big house is the only building I see. I know this big house flowing though my eyes is called a building. Yet it's the only building I have ever seen. I'm not really sure how I learned to do it, but I can name everything I see and hear. It makes me feel better. Sometimes I wonder what it would be like if all the things that pass before me would stream into my eyes without changing into words. I would never understand a thing. It would be bad.

I've always been standing in these same footsteps in this same place. I don't know why. I try not to pay it much thought. I know it has always been like this and will probably stay like this for the rest of my life. It's not wise to think about it too much. It can't be changed. Instead I concentrate on the things I see and can name. But sometimes it isn't enough and I start thinking about myself. It's dangerous, I know, but what I see and hear is always the same. It isn't always enough. But I try not to think too much. It's not safe.

The walls of the building are white and its windows seem black from where I'm standing. If I gaze at the building for some time the divisions between the walls and the windows get blurred. The roof of the big house is red. In front of it there's a low hill which rolls along till it stops at my feet. I'm standing on a neatly cut lawn. I know the grass is soft, although I can't touch it. The grass doesn't grow. It has always been neatly cut. Sometimes my feet get very tired.

There's a flagpole close by me. The flagstring slaps against the hard wood of the staff. There is no flag. On the lawn a light breeze is always blowing. The clicking of the thread beating against the pole never stops. It has always been like this. It doesn't annoy me. I don't notice the clicks unless I want to think about them.

Sometimes I'm very tired. My arms, legs, body, face and lips are tired – especially my lips. But it's no use feeling tired. It can't change anything. It's best to try to forget. I must forget how tired I am. I blow. I have been blowing for a very long time. Sometimes my lips tickle, but I mustn't think about it. I have to keep blowing. I feel the water at my lips. I feel the pressure of the mouthpiece against my teeth. The coils of the tuba wrap themselves around me, pressing against my body. I have to keep on blowing. If I don't I'll drown. I mustn't stop. Above my head I hear the splashing of the water which fills the tuba and presses against my lips. If the air in my lungs runs out the splashing will stop. Everything would stop. But it mustn't stop. If I were to stop blowing the water would force its way into my mouth, down my throat and fill my lungs.

Wilhelm Emilsson

I mustn't think about it. I continue to blow. I've still got air.

But sometimes I'm very tired. My feet are stuck. The whole of my body is stuck. The only part of it I can move are my eyes. They ache. I'm unable to blink. I have no eyelids. The only thing I can do is breathe out. Sometimes I can't help worrying that perhaps one day I won't be able to do it anymore. I can breathe out, but I can't breathe in.

As far as I know I've always been standing on exactly this spot. Yet a few times – it happens very rarely – something seems to stir behind the here and now. Fragments of something which perhaps was once a whole picture light up for a few seconds. I am walking. I stop and touch a wall with my hand. And I am walking. I feel smaller than I am now, closer to the grass. The next bit is larger then the other two. I place my hand on a wall. My other hand is enclosed in warmth. This sensation lasts long enough for me to be almost certain that it isn't something I'm making up. Someone bigger than me is holding my hand and telling me what is on the other side of the wall. Then the light dies. If I'm lucky the remembrance repeats itself – I'm almost certain that it is a remembrance. But I never recall anything else. And it occurs very rarely. I believe the person holding my hand was my father and that we had been standing by one of the walls of the white building. It must have been he who taught me the words for the things I see and hear. I often try to remember what it was he told me was on the other side of the wall. But I can't. When the fragments come alive it doesn't matter. While it lasts I know that it was he who taught me to name things, and I'm proud and convinced that it was he as well who handed me the tuba and told me to blow. For a few warm moments everything has meaning and I know why I'm blowing. Everything is a beautiful picture. With me in its centre.

But then a bulge appears in the top corner. A rusty iron nail punches a slit in the canvas. It forces its way downward, ripping the picture into bits. The threads of the fragments flap in the wind and once again there is nothing but the clicks of the line beating against the flagpole and the splashing of the water in the tuba above me. During those moments I'm almost convinced that I never had a father. Fathers don't leave their sons tied down like dogs to the same spot. Fathers don't abandon their sons.

My heartbeat quickens. Something is going on. Two men come out of the white building. They disappear and I begin to wonder whether perhaps they were an illusion. Then they reappear and walk towards me. They wear white robes and carry stethoscopes around their necks. I see them smile. They stand before me, nod at each other and smile again. They act as if I'm not like them, as if I were a thing. I'm not quite certain what is happening, but I know something is wrong. I'm afraid. One of the men has a colourful packet in his hand. Again they nod and the one with the packet raises it. My eyes follow the movement of his hand. He starts to pour out the contents of the packet. A white cloud appears and although I can no longer see it I know he is emptying the packet into the tuba. I'm scared. Yet at the same time I can't help wondering how I know the names of all these strange new things. I even know what was in the packet: washing powder. Now it's in the tuba, mixing with the water. The soap burns my lips. Bubbles stream out of the tuba carrying my last breaths away from my lungs. I can't blow any more. I feel the burning taste of soap in my mouth, my nose, my throat. Why did . . . ? Why did they . . . ?

.

Under glaring lights, the tuba player lay on an operating table surrounded by green plastic curtains. The men in the white robes had made certain he was dead. A scream came through the curtains.

'Cut it out,' grumbled one of the doctors.

'There is a woman having a baby in here,' a stern, authoritative voice answered.

'Don't go out of your depth, assistant nurse,' replied the doctor, grinning to his colleague.

'Assistant! I'll let you know you're not talking to any assistant. I'm a nurse. And don't imagine I'll put up with . . .'

'For heaven's sake. People are trying to work in here.'

'Trying to work . . . Here is a woman having a baby and you . . .'

'Of course. Of course. We've heard it all before.' The doctor had lost interest in the quarrel.

The screams increased.

The broken eyes of the tuba player stared into the harsh lights above the dissecting table. Dried soap rills could be seen under his nostrils and at the corners of his mouth. The doctors handled their scalpels eagerly.

'What a pair of lungs he must have,' said one of them. He was getting ready to make the first incision. His hand trembled a little.

'Unbelievable,' whispered the other. The doctor placed a gloved hand on the tuba player's naked breast. The scalpel slid across soft pale skin. A red line followed in the wake of the glittering steel.

A low clicking sound was heard as the corpse's eyes popped out of their sockets. They glided majestically towards the lights – each in its own rainbow-coloured bubble of soap. More bubbles followed from the blackness of the gaping sockets. The doctors dropped their knives and backed slowly away from the tuba player. They watched the staring pair of eyes move in the direction of the plastic curtain. The doctors waited with grimaced faces. When the eyes finally edged over the curtain dark moans escaped from their dry throats.

There had been a slight lull in the woman's screams. The red and bloated body of a child was halfway into the world. The woman was urged to make her final effort.

The two doctors decided not to stay on for the real screaming to begin. They walked away.

Michelle Heinemann

A Canadian writer, Michelle Heinemann has recently
completed her first collection of short stories. She works as
an editor and television producer in Calgary, Alberta.
Her fiction and non-fiction have been published
extensively in magazines in Canada.

Singing

one

Doe, a dear, a female dear

The thing I really need to get at is why do you change the way you do so suddenly? First you are singing with me, as loud and as happy as can be. Then you sing less and seem to get the words confused. I can see you building up ready to pop the goo out of your left ear, squirt it out. On the wall it looks like dead spiders flattened and brown and running down.

In your part of the room there are lots of squirts on the wall. I used to be able to see them, all brown and waxy, but that was before Hector threw cleaning acid in my face. He said I was a lazy cow that I didn't clean the wall. He said I was such a lazy cow if I didn't smarten up I'd never see a quart of milk again. Ever. I said, No I wouldn't clean the wall. It's true. Now I'll never see a quart of milk again.

My skin burned so hard for days. Later it oozed. Now it's thin and scaly, scabbed. My eyes are like that too. I scratch at them and they bleed. Hector keeps coming around saying, Too bad I can't see much, but it's a good thing I didn't die. He says he needs two for what he wants, it's no good with just one. He says he wants us to sing for him. That's the one thing he says over and over. The other things he says just sometimes, like what he said to Jeana before he hit her against the wall because she messed it up. He yelled out at her that she never listened to him.

Hector never tries anything with sex on either of us never at all, but we never know if he might. He really mostly wants us to sing for him. So we sing something easy for Jeana because she's nearly deaf. *'Doe a dear.'* Whenever he hits me, I sing louder, absolutely as loud as I can. You would've thought he'd have cut my vocal cords.

two

Ray, a drop of golden sun

The way I keep my senses now is just to sing all the time. Sometimes before when I could still see I would close my eyes and think of Ted and I being close in bed under the covers. My Ted, my husband, my life is with Ted and I still want him to love me the way he knows how. So I think of a time like that with Ted and I sing and sing, lots of singing, singing all the time. *'Doe a dear, a female dear, ray, a drop of golden sun.'*

Jeana used to sing along. That was before she squirted her brains out. It was too late for me to see that, though. 'Doe, ray. *Ray, a drop of golden sun.'*

Each day before I couldn't see and when Jeana could still hear she'd asked me how she looked. She was odd about that. Each day, just once, she'd ask me if she was still beautiful and it was all I could do to lie. Jeana was used to being looked at, she had told me a few stories of that before Hector popped her brains. Now I can no longer see her but she tells me she looks different. Hector has a radio and Jeana tells me she can see herself in the clear plastic part of it. Each day she says her neck is getting redder and the side of her face a bit more dark purple. I don't remember it as dark purple at all, so that part is hard to imagine, and it doesn't really matter much to me. I can only see what is already in my mind. I can no longer see new things. I think it's just as well, because I know seeing Jeana's face when brain goo blows out her ear would surely be one of the awful things.

You should have heard the scream that came from her. All of a sudden she screamed so that I could hear it against my eyes. Now there is no one for me to sing with.

Unless Hector of course.

three

Me, a name I call myself

I'm surprised Jeana can sing as well as she can, as close to key and as loud as she does. It must be the same for her that we remember things already in our minds so she can still sing them. I don't think I could teach her to sing a song she's never heard before, but she knows this one well. '*Me, a name I call myself.'*

The only thing wrong is her singing is flat. She is a little tone-deaf, but sometimes she sings just perfect and then all of a sudden she veers way off, but it doesn't last too many notes and she's back on the tone again and I just ignore all that and sing on and on as loud and as gaily as I can. 'Doe, ray, me. *Me, a name I call myself.'* My name is Marnie.

Before when Hector would start down the wooden stairs Jeana and I could be doing such different things. She might be brushing her hands through her hair. I might be smoothing the wrinkles out of my clothes. But as soon as Hector put one foot on the steps, we stopped whatever it was we were doing and started to sing. We sang as loudly as we could and even when Hector brought only bread and tea we kept singing.

'*Me, a name I call myself.'* At first Jeana didn't sing with me, she just called out instead for her Joseph, but Hector knocked her extra hard then, so soon she didn't do it much anymore. The best thing was just to keep singing. He didn't hurt her as bad that way. I never said anything about Ted.

four

Far, a long long way to run

This is not me in prison maybe in Israel or South Africa. I didn't know a whole lot about everything there is to know in the world before. But Hector has a radio and he never turns it off. I hear the news all the time. I've remembered what is going on wrong in the world. But I never heard that I was missing. I am simply Marnie walking to the store for a quart of milk. I was running really, because my little girl Debra was being looked after by the neighbours, so I hurried. Debra is three now, she's a real singer. I taught her, starting when she was around eighteen months. Deb, I said, let's sing, you'll like it. 'Doe, ray, me, fa,' I sang and she sang, 'Doe, way, me, me, me, me, me, me,' until Ted would pick her up and whirl her around.

Somebody jumped out from behind the trees and hit me with something. *Far, a long long way to run.'* Now I don't know where I am. I can't see, but even when I could, all I could see was I was lying on bare ground and there were high dirt walls all around me. No windows, and just a bit of light from the stairhole in the ceiling so I could see the stairs were wooden. But I never heard movement above us. That was one of the odd things.

five

Sew, a needle pulling thread

Across the room in a pile on the ground is Jeana. When Hector brought me down the steps and into the dirt room I was out cold. Jeana told me this was so and that Hector said finally he's got enough here to work with. He said it takes two to sing the way he likes, that's what Jeana said and later Hector said it too, over and over. He pulled me across the floor to Jeana, gave her a needle and some thread and told her to sew me. That she told me too, but I came to long before the rip was healed and took the thread out because the rip needed to bleed. 'Doe, ray, me, far, sew.'

Jeana figured nobody has found her yet because Hector got a two-day start. Where she worked they wouldn't likely phone her until she'd been away a day and she says Joseph was helping his father at the lake until Friday, so he'd never know. She says she's not surprised to hear that we are not on the news. '*Sew, a needle pulling thread.*'

She is simply Jeana, with her computer entry job, her own apartment and her boyfriend who might marry her some day. Hector grabbed her at an alley just before dusk. She was leaving from visiting her girlfriend and she was going to her car. He smashed her face on the left side. 'Doe, ray, me, far, sew. *Sew, a needle pulling*' Jeana said she never saw it, the only thing she did see was Hector. She saw the terror in his eyes and she saw him yelling at her, screaming out, 'You never listen to me,' over so many times she said she thought it was going to make her throw up.

Jeana's situation was advanced by the time I came to. Her ear squirts every day and when that happens her eyes go inward and she gags. Afterwards, she comes over to my side and sits on the bare ground beside me and we hold hands and sing. 'Doe, doe, me, me, sew, sew, far, far, ray, ray.' We've tried other songs, but maybe her ear is starting to make her forget a whole lot; because she gets the words on this one right only sometimes now, and gets the tunes and the words to the other songs we try so confused we forget what we are singing. 'Doe, a dear pulling thread. Far, a long way to the sun. Me, a drink for female dears. Sew, how fast can you run?'

<h3 style="text-align:center">six</h3>

Lah, a note to follow sew

When my bleeding came I was happy, since Ted and me got reckless a few times and there was a doubt in my mind it would come. It's odd though that before with my bleeding I would need to double over in cramps and lay on the hot water bottle. Now I think I don't have that anymore or at least I don't remember that I doubled over and got hot water. I maybe did ask Hector for something, brought it to his attention because he stayed over me the whole time with his fingers all caught in my hair to swing my head, saying over and over again to stop, that I was making a mess – and Hector hated messes – I should stop being a lazy cow again and make things nice for Hector and sing, '*Lah, a note to follow sew.*'

This time I wanted to not have Hector think I was a lazy cow anymore, so I would have stopped if only I could. That was the odd part, was that this time I sure wanted to do as Hector said but there was no way I could. I just kept up on the singing, kept singing, singing, and then Hector asked me where I learned that nice song I always sang. 'Doe, ray, me, far, sew. *Lah, a note to follow.*'

Singing

Jeana didn't have her time. I think it popped out her ear.

seven

Tea, a drink with jam and bread

I started singing first by myself. Jeana wasn't in on it, just me singing to my little girl Debra who I was hurrying for because she was at the neighbours'. *'Tea, a drink with jam and bread.'* That was about the next day after I came to and had pulled Jeana's sewing out of my head. I can't say it was a big surprise or anything when she came over to me and started singing too. *'Doe, a dear pulling thread. Far, a long way to the sun. Me, a drink for female dears. Sew, how fast can you run? Tea for me.'*

Before that she was sniffling in the corner about Joseph but she figured in time, with Hector, that she should try to put Joseph out of her mind. So we sang. We managed to learn the tune fairly well by the time Hector hit her for getting a few words mixed up. That was also an odd thing of Hector's, to hit us except if we were singing exactly right. He liked it when we sang right.

Now I sing all the time except for the brief naps I take every hour to refresh myself. Since Jeana's brains squirted all over the wall, I have stayed awake around the clock, staggering short naps all the time so as to keep Hector confused about when I am awake or not. If I am asleep, he will hurt me more. He comes by now and says I sing like a dead fish, without the other one I sound nearly finished. I say, Yes I know it's too bad, if he would consider singing with me maybe we could make it sound good again. I have him so puzzled and after a few days he begins to sing. It's bad at first, so off key and missing notes but it took a few days of that before he could get the sounds better. *'Doe, ray, me, far, sew, lah, tea.'*

I didn't care, he's happier when he sings so he won't hurt me as bad. *'Doe, a dear, a female dear. Ray, a drop of golden sun. Me, a name I call myself. Far, a long long way to run. Sew, a needle pulling thread. Lah, a note to follow sew. Tea, a drink with jam and bread.'*

eight

And that brings us back to doe, doe, doe, doe

The thing I really need to get at is why do you change the way you do so sud-

57

denly? First you are singing with me, as loud and as happy as can be. 'Doe, doe, doe, doe.' Then when you stop I hear only the radio, so I hear lots of snatches of the news. It's another thing that's so odd about what's happened, is we've never been on the news. They don't know that Jeana is dead and that I can't see any more. I don't know what is known, but it's not this.

Now Hector wants to sing again. Sometimes he'll just be singing, singing as loud as can be 'Doe, ray, me, far, sew, lah, tea, doe' and then there is silence and then maybe he'll hit me or give me some tea and I never know which it will be.

Rolf Hughes

Rolf Hughes was born in 1963. He gained a first class
honours degree in English from York University in
1988 and a distinction in the MA in Creative Writing
at the University of East Anglia in 1989. He is
currently writing a novel while pursuing a doctorate in
Creative and Critical Writing at East Anglia, where he
teaches prose fiction on the undergraduate programme.
His work has appeared on BBC radio and in
publication by Faber and Faber. In this story he quotes
from *Refrain* is taken from a five story cycle set over
twenty-four hours

Refrain

The Death of Seduction

'This is it,' Synovia said, flipping on a light and closing the front door behind her. 'Home sweet home. Make yourself comfortable.' She slipped out of her coat, tossed it onto a chair, and clipped her short black hair back from her face. 'I suppose you want a drink. Jim's got some lager. You must replace it, okay? That's the deal.'

Wax edged into the room, sat on the nearest piece of furniture and nodded solemnly. Synovia disappeared through a sliding white door into a kitchen leaving Wax, a dabbler in domestic anthropology, to take in his surroundings. They revealed upper-lower-middle-class or lower-upper-middle-class aspirations, depending on perspective. He was sitting on a leather, or a good imitation, settee. He liked leather: his jacket was leather, genuine black leather, multi-zipped and jangling with skulls. The sofa stuck to him like a suction-pad. It would hold him in place, he found himself thinking, when he was underneath. He was, if anywhere, invariably underneath. At his feet was a sheep fleece made of white nylon. He made a mental note about this. Static. Hair-raising. Kinky. Opposite, a gas fire with plastic coal; above it – was that Garbo staring from a framed collage on the wall? She was crowded by a multitude of cut-up women including, prominently, Monroe or Debby Harry or Madonna – it was a grainy reproduction and Wax couldn't quite decide in his present state. He lost himself in the smiling grey eyes of the multiplying stars.

'Put a record on!' Synovia called from the kitchen, her voice cavernous in the refrigerator. 'Diana Ross or Billie Holiday. Nothing too weird.' Wax tried to raise himself, but the sofa seemed to have him in its jaws. He took his jacket off and pushed his backside slowly up from the brown upholstered gums which gently released him with a long, low sigh. Outside a motorbike whined closer and closer, then flashed past with a noise like a flying pneumatic drill. Wax flipped through the records on the shelf by the television set, ticking off each cover as it appeared. It was getting to the point, he thought, where he could predict not just the content, but even the order of a collection like this: The Eagles, surprise, surprise . . . yes, Elton John . . . where's Joan Armatrading? Aha, tucked behind Fleetwood Mac's *Rumours*, where else? A record would give them twenty minutes on the sofa before he had to get up and turn it over. Not a great idea. He crossed the room towards the kitchen.

'Listening to records, it's a seance, isn't it? Ghosts on the vinyl, come on down, invitation-only . . . Problem is, I wouldn't invite any of the ghouls in your collection.' But Synovia had gone into the room beyond the kitchen, from where there was the sound of running water and then the larger gush of a flushing toilet. Wax returned to the sofa. He blew onto his hand and smelled his breath. Not too bad, all things considered. He stared at the unlit fire, scratching first his ear then, surreptitiously, his crotch.

'So much for the knees-up, then,' Synovia said, returning to the room with an unopened can of beer and a steaming cup. 'There's your drink.' She put the can on the mantelpiece between a blue cut-glass swan and a clock without numbers, and sat in the room's only armchair, her hands cradling the cup. 'I'm not complaining. I get headaches standing behind the bar while you lot play.'

'Thanks.' Wax reached across for the can, ripped it open, tipped it to his mouth and took several large gulps. 'Keep music live,' he paused to say. 'That's my union motto, only I'm not a member. Cheers.' He upended the can again, closed his eyes in concentration, then flourished the empty tin in mid-air and wiped his lips with the back of his hand. 'I'll replace it.' The telephone rang twice then was silent. Synovia shrugged.

'Happens all the time,' she said. 'We're only one digit different from the cinema.'

'All the weirdos after the late show, eh?' Synovia shrugged again and stared down at the cup in her hands. 'Wonder if there's any horror on TV.' Wax's words were now slurring themselves. 'A late night spooker.'

'Have a look if you want,' Synovia replied, standing up. 'I'm going to bed.' By way of preparation she had changed into a dragon-patterned dressing-gown.

'Can I just check?' he asked hastily.

'If you must,' she replied, flopping back into the armchair with a sigh. 'I suppose I'll have a look before I go.'

*

There was a studio discussion on the state of the nation, a torpid game of snooker, a testcard with a relentless whine: no 'late night spooker'. Cable TV saved the day. Synovia and Wax were slouched halfway down their separate pieces of the would-be three-piece, competing against an androgyne with purple hair extensions, the 'special guest' of an all-night music show comprising videos and interviews with special guests.

' . . . *Sorry, Mike, my private life is not up for discussion. I mean, people, like, assume it's part of the job, all the chicks and that, and, well, on tour, that's something else. But, as you know, I haven't toured for, like, four years . . .*'

'What a prick,' Synovia said.

'Sssh,' Wax said, avid for moral guidance.

'*Generally, yeah, all my energy goes into my music. I write all the videos. It's hard to say where my songs come from. I guess it's a talent that you're born with. No, I don't have any, like, influences. Not that I can think of. Experience, I suppose. Well, yeah, Life. When something really gets me it leaves a scar, a deep scar, Mike, one that . . . never heals.*'

'Sounds like acne,' Synovia said, glancing sideways at Wax. 'This guy is tragic.'

The young interviewer in his earnest black polo neck and low-key suit leaned towards the rock star and sucked thoughtfully on his pen.

'*Many of the songs on your new album deal with . . . well, sex. Do songs like "Do Me Like I Like You To" indicate a reaction on your part against the sort of self-sanitizing society we live in, with its fear of sex and hysterical reduction of the body to the quality of its fluids? Is that song an admission that the lyrical love song, or indeed the raunchy anthem of lust, is no longer valid in a world where pleasure is a gamble against viral contamination and where desire is thus relegated, as in adolescence, to solo "out-of-body" experiences?*'

'*Yeah.*' The rock star nodded his headpiece in a vigorous cascade of colour. '*The song is addressed to me, Mike, yeah.*'

'*Candid stuff,*' the host said, addressing the camera. '*And there's more after the break.*'

'Total wanker,' Synovia said, exhaling smoke as she leaned back against the armchair's shoulder. '*Ex-per-ience, Mike, and hee, hee, Life – these are what influ-ence me* . . . What about you, Wax? What gets you going?'

'Dunno.' Wax picked his ear and chewed it over. 'Dope. Leather. Myself. What about you?'

Synovia glanced around the room and stretched a leg, splitting the dressing-gown. 'Mmmm . . . Marilyn . . . Billie . . . Jimmy Dean . . .'

Wax groaned. 'Wheel out the stiffs! How about Jim Morrison?' he offered helpfully. 'Jimi Hendrix? Sid 'n' Nancy?'

'Ugh!' Synovia flinched and passed a hand over her forehead. 'Save me!'

'*. . . I'm lost in dreams . . . I'm a shadow in a dream world . . . and holding hands won't help me any more!*'

The rock star strummed a red guitar and mimed along to his latest single on a yellow beach, against a cloudless blue horizon on which even the billowing grey clouds of a simulated atomic explosion acquired a form of desensitised beauty.

'What of the living then?' Wax asked, his eyes flicking down to the white flesh in the parted dressing-gown. 'Like, who turns you on, baby?' Synovia stared long and hard at him before replying, 'The latest man. If it's any good.'

Rolf Hughes

I want you to want me
To do me like I like you to

'Let's see what else is on,' Wax said, rising with an effort from the cloying grip of the leather gums.

'What's wrong with you?' Synovia caught him by a thigh-high rip in his black jeans and pulled him back towards her armchair. 'I thought you wanted . . .'

'I did.' Wax mumbled. 'I mean, nothing's wrong with me. I'm in demand, you know. Got to keep my strength up.'

'Oh God!' Synovia released him, turning pale. 'Have you got something to tell me? Some problem? Some place you'd rather be?' Wax turned away. 'There's nothing wrong with *that*, you know,' Synovia continued, her voice becoming more and more exasperated. 'All you had to do was tell me. Save wasting my time.'

'Listen,' Wax murmured to the misted front window. 'That's not it. I'm clean. And straight.' He turned to face her, gathering courage. 'I mean, I'm a highly-sought-after drummer, yes.'

'I see . . . So I'm lucky to 'ave got this booking?' She was out of her dressing-gown in a blink and stood, naked, facing him. 'Well?' She put her arms on his shoulders and pressed one knee softly into his groin. 'What's the problem?'

'Listen.' Wax reached across and turned the sound down on the television set.

Rain had started dripping onto the windowpane. Distantly, a series of car doors were being opened and slammed. Cries and laughter. More slamming. An engine revving. The clapper-clap-clat of high heels tottering precariously past. A chorus of neighbourhood dogs began baying across the grids of terraced housing, sending – who knows? – dog gossip through the night, despite backyard walls, steel collars, chains.

Wax took Synovia's smooth face in his hands, and fixed his bloodshot gaze on her large brown eyes.

'Don't hurry me. Why hurry? Who's hustling who? You or me? Mmmm? It's great, us two. Just as we are. No hassle.' He traced the thin lines of her pencilled eyebrows with his two index fingers. 'Wow, what brows! Little wisps of smoke. I like the way you make yourself up. Don't rush this. I've got to remember these brows, and, like, maybe much more. Mmm, I've got a very big memory.' His middle fingers traced the delicate curves and folds of her ears. 'No earrings. Yes, I like that. You hold yourself well. You don't need them. You're too natural. You're good with make-up. You could be an actress. You've got the face.' He leaned back to take her all in. 'No, on second thoughts, you're not cut out for it. Don't sell out, you're all you've got.' Sliding the palms of his hands over her cheeks, over her cheekbones, his fingers gliding over her temples and slipping through her hair, he closed his eyes, leaned his forehead against hers and continued in a barely audible whisper: 'Don't close your ears to your own special music. Inside you. You'll hear it. Just listen. But don't . . .'

'Don't lecture me!' Synovia jerked away, bumping against the armchair and sending it reeling backwards on its casters. She pulled on her dressing-gown, tied the cord in an angry knot around her waist and accidentally stepped on the long-lost TV remote control, whose sub-armchair hibernation was abruptly terminated in a puff of dust and a surge of sound from the hitherto mute television.

'Does-it-make-you-feel good . . .' she hollered above the squealing, churning music, 'to-sound-off? Makes-you-feel-*manly*, huh? Any-old-shit-as-long-as-you're-speaking-it's-all-pearls-of-wisdom-dribbling-from-your-gob . . .' She found the remote control and dropped the volume several decibels. 'That's it, isn't it? That's how you think!' Wax's eyes flitted to the TV screen which depicted a thrash band thrashing black guitars in an aesthetically-littered alleyway. Every time the chorus came round the singer, bald and bullworkered, leaned and leered point-blank at the camera:

Take a week's worth of ex-cre-tia
Smear it on your face - Oi!
Now you're nice and ready
To belong to the human race

'I don't know what to say,' he said.

'Shock me,' Synovia said. 'Say something original.'

Wax bit his lip and frowned at his feet. Synovia stared at him, resisting with difficulty the urge to punch, kick, and push him out of her house. A smile was slowly spreading across his face. He nodded to himself, cleared his throat and in a booming voice began reciting:

'*Oh gride on and dremmer!*' He gazed at her, his eyes shining triumphantly. '*Glem so and . . .* err . . . *durb . . .*'

'Jesus Christ, you're unreal!' She passed a hand over her face. This was her own time, her free time, it was supposed to be about pleasure, picking up a few signs, nothing simpler. Why wasn't he playing along? She should never have slipped off her dressing gown: he had her now. 'Trust me to pick another bloody musician,' she said, her voice falling into a minor key. 'They never know what to say. Or they never say the right things. Or even when they say the right things, they say them wrongly. Nothing changes. Thanks for walking me home. Now please, piss off. I've had enough.'

'Let's start again.' Wax said, holding out a reconciliatory hand.

'Goodnight.' Synovia turned and swept up the stairs. She paused to point for his benefit. 'The sofa's there and the door's there. Take your pick, but don't let me see you in the morning.'

Benson 'n' Hedges are always too thin
I need Capstan 'Full Strength' to get the tar in!
Cos I wanna be a beagle in an experiment lab
I wanna get cancer with my fags . . .

The thrash band ran riot over an elaborate labyrinth of conveyor belts in what was supposed to resemble a tobacco factory. Burning cigarettes protruded from every available hole in the singer's face; the bassist blundered around wearing the head of a giant beagle costume into whose velvet and cardboard jaws were crammed the gaily-coloured packets of the market-leading brands; the two other members of the band were content to stretch their faces to their leeriest extents and throw handfuls of cigarettes at the camera.

·

Wax sat in the dark room, staring at the flickering images on the television set with the volume turned down. The loss of sound did not seem to detract from the music videos: in most cases, if anything, silence enhanced the visuals. As the hours ticked by and the neighbourhood finally settled down to the long slumber of early morning, he found the same videos were coming up with monotonous regularity. The addition of the accompanying music would have made them unbearable.

Towards three in the morning, his eyes glazed on the nth repeat of the purple-haired rock star with his red guitar and tight grip of the ornamental microphone, Wax heard the springs of a mattress creak overhead, then the sound of bare feet padding around the bedroom, Synovia's presumably, it was all speculation now: out onto wooden floorboards, the landing, a pause, then across they went into the other room, the spare room perhaps? or Jim and Kim's, since they were out camping and stripping as usual. He heard a click, the sound of a telephone dial, a long number, international maybe . . . the sister in Hollywood? What time was it in Hollywood? A few moments silence, waiting . . . Then he heard Synovia's voice, low and confiding, the monotone of one not expecting to be interrupted. Wax strained his ears but could hear nothing. He tried to re-focus his attention on the silent videos. He sat through an epic minute of a starry-eyed model in a nineteen twenties flapper dress, throwing champagne glasses from a moonlit Brooklyn Bridge . . . The steady murmur, meanwhile, continued upstairs. Wax suddenly remembered the telephone on the kitchen counter, sighted on one of his innumerable trips to the toilet. It was three in the morning: who was she speaking to? What sort of person would never interrupt on the other end of the line? Curiosity lifted him from the sighing sofa, sent him across the room on tiptoe, eased back the sliding door and raised the earpiece to his ear, without waking the cat in its basket and without Synovia, upstairs, hearing a thing.

Imagine all the crossed lines of all the telephone networks in all the early-morning world concentrated onto one single line of hysterical non-communication; such was the sound of the 'Party Line' that our hero now heard for the first time. Wax couldn't believe his ears. He often suspected they were less than one hundred percent hi-fidelity, and luckily had his own private ritual for such crises. He took the phone from his ear, rubbed his eyes, extracted a cotton bud from one of the many zip pockets in his jacket, cleaned out his left ear, examined the now discoloured tip of the tiny plastic stick, and dropped it into an empty beer can. The little finger of his right hand sported a long, pointed nail. He now used it to probe deep within his auditory canal for any remaining traces of his namesake which, ever since the onset of puberty and (coincidentally) his passion for drumming, had regularly formed a final wall of defence over his inner drum. He snapped his fingers. Clear as a bell. Satisfied, he tentatively returned the phone to his left ear. Still, the same babble of voices, distorted, difficult to untangle. Synovia's voice alone was calm, an intimate whisper amidst the disembodied shrieks and jeers of the raging male assembly.

' . . . waiting to speak to you *all day.* I can no longer remember what my friends look like, and I can't imagine what you look like. It's hard to tell from the voices . . .

'Hard! I'm hard! Just for you!'

' . . . *My name's Roy. Roy! Roy! I'm not queer. I'm not a fucking queer! My girlfriend's next door. Suspenders and stilettoes . . .'*

' . . . So spread the word, invite them to join our little party. I *love* making new friends. We should all come together . . .'

'Come, come, come together! Yeeaahh! All over your face!'

'. . . A common heart beating in all these different bodies . . . '

'Yeeeah! Bodies!'

'She's reading the script!'

'Tell me, baby, tell me . . .'

'Danny, is that you? Danny?'

'Aaaaah, Steve, ram-rod Steve, the stock-car king of . . . I'm doing ninety down the high street! It's Steve here, Steve the ram-rod, the stock-car king of Harlesden. Who's the bird? Who's talking dirty tonight?'

'*Ray, try it! Just try it! I'll do anything, Ray, anything, any time . . .*'

'*Roy! Not Ray! Roy! Roy!*'

' . . . Picture this, my . . . friends. No more lonely nights. Cold sheets. No more one-cup teabags. Joyless fingers. No more lying awake, wrapped in cold sheets . . .'

'Shit!'

' . . . turning grey. . . quietly greying . . . Fading . . .'

'*Hey fruitcake! Do you fuck?*'

' . . . No more doorbolts and spy-holes . . .'

'*She'll hold a collection next . . .*'

'No more lace curtains drawn against the world and settling over dreams like... like . . . like a death shroud . . .'

'*I – can – SEE – you! I'm on my car phone. I'm watching you . . .*'

'*Where's the party? Where's the party? Where's the party, I've got a hard-on!*'

'So? I've got nothing on. That what you want? Well it's true. This is my . . . body. Mine! I own it!'

'*Yeeaaah!*'

'*Tell me baby . . . Tell me about it. Tell me how you feel.*' Murmuring middle-aged voice. Loud enough to be a local caller . . .

The sudden silence made Wax start guiltily. He put a hand over the mouthpiece so Synovia could not hear his breathing. Red eyes were staring at him from the ballooning reflection of his face in the electric kettle. His heart was jumping around his chest.

'How do I feel?' Synovia's voice was low and heavy upstairs. The kitchen ceiling creaked with its weight.

'*How do you feel, baby?*' Silence flooded across the Party Line, spread across every network, filled every terminal and silenced momentarily every Party Liner. There was a click as the receiver fell onto the hooks, and then the monotonous growl of a dead line.

.

'Wake up!' The curtains are open, sunlight streams into the room and frames the silhouette of Synovia who is dressed and standing with folded arms next to the sofa. 'Get up! I've got to go to work, the others will be back soon and they won't want to find you here.'

Wax rubs his eyes. He stretches his legs and raises his head from the folded jacket which has served as a pillow and left a zip imprint deep in his cheek.

'Wha –?'

Refrain

'Get up!'
He gets unsteadily up.

•

There was a blur of activity on the street as neighbours wordlessly set about their morning activities. The road had become a battlefield for parking territory. A history of neighbourhood rivalries, jealousies, infidelities could be read in the long line of scratched and dented cars. Daily feuds continued after dark. Each morning, drivers mournfully inspected the latest damage. Neighbours. Everybody needs good neighbours. The Neighbourhood Watch watched their suspicious neighbours from look-out points in the dark bank of terraces. This was a 'good' side of town, a *desirable* quarter. Good fences make good neighbours.

Synovia set a brisk pace, Wax kept up; they walked in silence, dodging the rain-dripping trees, taking pleasure in the sound of wet tyres on the tired tarmac. They took a detour over a disused railtrack, counting the condoms between the sleepers. They passed hospital railings on which an ambulance driver in shirtsleeves hung his head. They pressed on towards the river and thence the town proper. Wax felt like skipping in the morning sunshine. Something had happened to him. His teeth kept spilling out between his lips. He was full of mischief and fun. He wanted to wave at the tourist cruisers then collapse on the riverbank and see how many passengers jumped to their feet in alarm. Synovia told him she was meeting someone before work, she did not want to be late. And no, Wax did not know him. Or her. And no, he could not come along too. Wax laughed aloud, his face radiating gratitude for the miracle in denim jacket and mini-skirt at his side. He should talk a little about himself; this, after all, was The Real Thing. He told her that he had only one pair of trousers, the ones he was wearing, black jeans with red lining. When he wore them with red turn-ups he was in a good mood, when he wore them as plain, black jeans he was not: that way, he said, he could dress to fit the mood even with just the one pair of trousers. Synovia glanced down. He had left his turn-ups turned down. She looked at his face. He was grinning again. So much for theory.

'Where are you going, Wax?' she asked, wondering whether science could isolate and eliminate the hormonal aberration responsible for this idiot shambling into her life.

'To the river,' he replied. 'With you. We're going to the river.' She shook her head in disbelief and increased her pace.

·

They did not stay long at the river. Instead of cruise ships lined with tourists, they found a pigeon, half-submerged, furiously flapping its wings. It was trying to escape the water, but was merely bobbing up and down, propelling itself slowly towards the shore. A group of spectators had gathered on the concrete bank and stood around with cans of beer, shouting encouragement, cracking jokes, placing bets even. The pigeon's strength was waning as it neared the bank. Its wings flopped and spread across the water. Synovia was about to lower herself into the river and wade across to save the bird, but the spectators talked her out of it. One put his arm around her and told her not to worry. It was only a pigeon. The river was crawling with all sorts of disease. Wax put his arm through hers and tried to lead her away, but she freed herself and ran across to pull a lifebelt from its hanging place on the riverside wall. The pigeon by this time was floating listlessly. Synovia lowered the lifebelt into the river, thread-ing the attached orange rope carefully through her hands. It bumped downstream, carried by the gentle current. She steered it until the motionless body of the pigeon drifted into the circle of plastic. She walked slowly along the edge of the bank, towing the bird to a raised platform where someone had tipped some rubble and rusting wire. The tiny island was an inch above the waterline, but the bird was incapable of clawing over this final obstacle to safety. Synovia tried to lift it with the lower curve of the lifebelt, but it re-peatedly slipped off the smooth plastic. Wax watched her struggling, and re-marked that the pigeon was dying or dead. As if in response, the pigeon's neck extended and stiffened, its beak gaped open, its eyes widened. On the river-bank a tall cluster of silhouettes stared with open mouths, and faded, and van-ished.

'Nice try, love. Eh, how 'bout saving my life next?'

'She can put a ring round me anytime!'

A renewed snapping of ring-pulls punctuated the laughter from the can-carrying crowd by the bank.

·

They climbed steps and crossed a silent car park, Synovia pale and subdued. She walked close to Wax, hoping he would steer her some place, hoping he would stop and embrace her, let her close her eyes and concentrate on her breathing. Above them, the sky pressed down like a sheet of scrap metal.

'It's bad news, animals dying,' Wax shook his head wistfully. He was enjoying himself in his new role. Love had crashed into his life like a sharp smash on the splash cymbal. It reverberated through his heart like a mighty drum roll trapped in a Watkins Copycat echo chamber. Synovia was so frail and vulnerable; she *needed* him. He glanced at her: yes, she needed him. 'I used to have a tortoise when I was young,' he continued. 'One day I came home and tried to feed it some dandelion leaves, but it wouldn't come out of its shell. So I picked it up and had a look inside. Guess what? It was swarming with ants. My mum told me it got stung in the eye by a wasp a few days before. She hadn't been able to bring herself to speak about it. Well, that fucked me up no end. Then we got a border collie. I called it Whippet because it had this expression like someone was about to whip it. It could run like the wind. One day it ran beneath the wheels of an ice cream van I was chasing. That fucked me up no end. Then, when I was eight . . .'

'Wax!' Synovia pleaded.

' . . . I was in a chip shop full of the local piss artists. They were pushing each other around and shouting at the girl behind the counter. I stayed by the door, trying not to be noticed, waiting for my turn. A cat walked in and brushed my legs. I knelt down and petted it. It was really, like, affectionate. Then it smelled the food. It jumped up onto the counter and strutted along the glass cabinet where they keep the fish warm. It was purring and its tail started twitching when it caught sight of all that fish. Rows and rows of the stuff, nice and golden. One of the blokes by the counter started stroking it. It arched its back but kept its eyes on the fish. He winked at the others, looked at me standing by the door, and said, 'Pussy, pussy, pussy,' to the girl behind the counter. I was shitting myself. Suddenly he picked the cat up and threw it into the vat of batter. It shrieked for a split second, then sank into the vat. The men ran from the shop. The girl sat down and stared at her feet. Then she stood up and put her hands over her mouth. I stood there holding my money, like I'd been sent for fried cat and chips. I was about to start crying, so I ran home. I was only eight. blubbering all the way. I didn't know what we were going to have for dinner. That fucked me up no end. I still dream about it. I can still hear the spit and hiss of that vat of batter . . .'

Wax tailed off, feeling all was not well with his companion. Perhaps he'd missed something out. 'You know,' he added, reaching for a philosophical note in his voice, 'after a while, you get used to these things.'

'Do you know what I like most about you, Wax?' Synovia asked, moving away from him as he leaned eagerly forward to listen. 'I mean, aside from your intelligence and good looks. It's your dazzling sense of humour, of course, your knack of making the world all sweetness and light. If you want sympathy, forget it.'

Wax took her hand. 'I care about animals,' he said quietly, squeezing her fingers and wondering how he might become all sweetness and light. 'And I care about . . .'

'Do me a favour, Wax.' They walked on in silence, sheltering within their own separate thoughts.

'Let's get something to eat,' Wax said, suddenly cheerful again. 'We should hold a wake for that drowned pigeon.'

They passed along the first of the shopping streets where people were walking with serious, intent expressions, with arms nailed to the ground by gaily-coloured carrier bags, with an abstracted grace to their movements. A small crowd had gathered outside one shop window. Faces were pressed against the glass, faces multiplied on a bank of TV screens stacked behind a home video camera, which was slowly rotating on a tripod, scanning the crowd, provoking waves of drooling desire. Wax caught a glimpse of himself on the top row of screens. He stopped and showed Synovia. He looked good with her.

Synovia's fingers were limp in his grip. She seemed indifferent to the pavement dramas all around her. In the pulse of her hand, Wax felt all responsibility transferred to himself. From hidden speakers high above the street a dozen violins played alternatively jaunty and soothing refrains. Wax led the way through the crowds. Today he was king of everything he saw. This was his high-spirited ballet. The shoppers swarmed through the festive shops in time to the muzak. Anything was possible. He turned off the high street and led Synovia through the long cool interior of a shopping arcade. It was a deserted boulevard of frozen elegance, with mannequins behind plate-glass windows twisted into surgical girdles, displays of cards, pink and heart-shaped, thermal socks, dartboards, yesteryear's hairstyles, a self-service haunted by pensioners, and a pond with goldfish floating over pale coins – specks of hope tossed, for luck, long ago. Wax often came to linger in the arcade and breath the sad polish of history. He liked the echo of footsteps rising to the glass canopy. He liked the lack of choice, the simple necessity of crossing from one end of the arcade to the other.

He was replaying Synovia's voice on the telephone the previous evening, over and over, the mysterious sermon he had heard in the kitchen. He could not connect that voice to the person at his side. He had now seen her naked, he'd seen her shaken by death – albeit pigeon-death – but he'd never known her so exposed, never so unguarded as the lonely voice that murmured on to anonymous listeners. He leaned against her as they walked, shoulder to shoulder on the wide marble floor. A bird fluttered around the glass canopy, each collision echoing through the empty arcade.

They turned onto the road that led to the centre of town. Traffic had come to a standstill. Vacant eyes stared from each car. Distantly, a siren wailed, a long howl of looped circuitry. A newspaper vendor huddled in a doorway, the headlines piled high at street level:

LOCAL THUGS CRACK SHOP SANTA'S SKULL

'Christmas already,' Wax murmured, glancing at Synovia. She seemed to be shrinking into her coat as he pulled her along.

'I have to meet someone,' she whispered, 'I can't be late.'

'We'll eat,' Wax said. 'You've got to eat.'

They crossed the road. The siren grew louder. They could see a police van wedged in the traffic ahead. As they neared it they saw it was empty, parked half on the pavement outside a department store, seemingly abandoned. Wax was transfixed by its rotating blue light, its piercing, monotonous wail. No one else was paying it the slightest attention. Suddenly the revolving glass doors of the department stores spat out three youths, one after the other. They sprinted across the road, leaped the park fence and tore across the grass in the direction of the bandstand. The door spun again and two uniformed policemen stumbled onto the pavement, through the traffic, and gave chase.

'No chance,' Wax murmured. 'Noooooo chance!' Now the door disgorged two more policemen and between them a sagging Father Christmas, beard hanging on by one hook, blood washing down his forehead.

They did not speak until they had walked some distance and left the siren far behind.

•

From a specialist sandwich shop in the centre of town Synovia bought a beef, prawn, and egg curry pie and Wax bought a peach and bacon sandwich and fed bits to the pigeons. They shared a carton of milk, which struck Wax as a sober and romantic choice. They were sitting on a bench in the square outside the municipal art gallery, facing a rectangle of glowing green water beneath the long defunct municipal fountain. On the right the civic headquarters rose up like a slab of icing, a mock Georgian frontpiece with white Roman columns and imitation marble steps. An office block sheltered behind the gleaming facade. Wax flipped a cigarette butt into the fountain. It touched the pool with a brief hiss, then disappeared – something had surfaced, swallowed it, and sunk back into its bilious underworld, leaving a couple of softly radiating circles over the glassy water.

'Guess what! There's something alive in there,' Wax said. Synovia stopped chewing and rewrapped her pie. Wax also stopped eating. A thought had suddenly occurred: after their picnic it would be a good time for their first kiss. He ran his tongue over his upper and lower teeth and surreptitiously checked his breath on the back of his hand. Not *too* bad, all things considered. But was Synovia in a kissing mood? Something was wrong. He could feel the distance between them. She had not said a word for some time. He could feel the tension in her limbs rippling along the wooden slats of the bench. He wanted to ask her about her telephone call in the early hours of the morning. But how could he put the question without giving himself away? And who was she meeting? Why wasn't she responding to the escalating rhythms of his heart?

From nowhere, a raincoat, a thick library book, and a thin man supporting both appeared before the bench and demanded money. Synovia started shaking. Wax stared at the man, then slowly unzipped one of the pockets in his jacket. The man's bones were bursting out of his face and his left forefinger ended in a stub above the middle joint. 'Twenty pence. Or pound coin. Pound coin . . .' His eyes flicked from Synovia to Wax and fastened on the hand inside the jacket pocket. 'Pound coin . . .' Rain fell, as if the clouds' underbelly had been finally slashed. 'Pound coin . . .'

'Here!' Wax threw a spray of loose change and watched the man rush pecking around the square as the coins rolled away in different directions. Wax put his arm around Synovia. She was still shaking. He squeezed her.

'It's okay,' he whispered. 'It's only foreign currency.'

She pushed him away and leaned free of his arm.

'I wish you hadn't done that,' she said quietly.

'I never know what to do,' Wax said. 'I mean, I feel bad either way, giving something or not, that's why I collect foreign coins. I suppose it makes no difference.'

'For God's sake, Wax! What's wrong with you? It makes all the fucking difference to him!'

Wax stared at her. She swore. Huh! So it was alright to swear now? 'I don't think so,' he said, scratching his ear thoughtfully. 'I don't see how you can say that. I mean, how can you know?' He looked at the finger that had been at his ear. 'Ah well, what the fuck!' he added.

'It makes a difference,' Synovia said again, lingering over the words. 'It makes all the difference.' She stood up and looked down at him. 'You've just got no idea, have you? What people do for money. What it does to them. We're not in a music video, Wax. Wake up, for Christ's sake!' Wax shrugged and folded his arms. Women always told him to wake up. One had even tried to help him along, after a gig, after a night of who-knows-what excesses. She slapped him across the side of his face with a beerglass. He couldn't remember her name. He thought of her being somewhere very dilapidated, in a damp room with no furniture, sitting in a corner thinking of him. This was the fate of everyone who misunderstood Wax. He sentenced them to eternal regret in a damp room in a condemned house on a crumbling street in a rainy town. And he forgot their names – partly by necessity, as there was already quite a crowd out there, wasting tearfully away, pining for him in their prison house of desolation.

A man crossed the square and approached them, grinning broadly at Synovia and shuffling into a few tap-dancing steps as he neared, all teeth and slitty smoker's eyes with crow's feet creasing the corners. He embraced Synovia then looked at Wax, a 'Who's-the-dick, chick?' expression on his face. Synovia introduced them, looking ill-at-ease. Danny Zimms was late forties, but wore jeans and biker's gear. His eyes were watery. One eyelid had a twitch. He smiled too much and wore gold on his fingers and neck. He told Synovia he had to be someplace in an hour. His smile conveyed infinite impatience. Wax's plans were in turmoil. He did not like seeing this smile used on Synovia. He did not want to hear this schedule. He wanted to believe they were involved in the moment, in the present, in their youth, him and Synovia, alone in the square without this creep.

'I have to go,' Synovia said. 'Sorry, Wax.' She looked, for a moment, as if she meant it.

Danny was chewing gum, his jaw roving round and round as he assessed Wax. 'See you around, chalky.' He winked and smiled. He turned to Synovia. 'Let's go, baby.' He lit a cigarette, took her arm, and they walked away.

'I'll call you tonight,' Wax shouted after her. 'Just to hear your sweet voice. I'm all sweetness and light on the phone. I'll call you up, don't you worry. I know how to get in touch.' But Synovia and Danny Zimms had crossed the busy street and had already disappeared amongst the hurrying raincoats.

•

Rain chainsawed the square. Puddles were shimmering with thousands of falling drops. Pigeons swarmed around the bench; they were bony and vicious, with greasy, rain-grey feathers, each eye a spot of black in an orange circle, and each set of claws hooking into the pavement as they pecked, scampered, and fought for the last crumbs of food.

Wax was slouched on the bench in the empty square, his long hair plastered to his skull, his foot flicking bits of pie to the agitated pigeons. 'Fuckers,' he said. 'Look at the state of you!' The traffic growled around the square. 'Lost your fucking voice, eh?'

The pigeons started to wander away. Wax threw the paper bag among them, then swooped and made a grab for the nearest. The bird darted out of reach, scurried to one side and captured a remaining lump of pastry. Wax flopped back onto the bench and stamped his foot with a loud slap on the streaming ground, making the birds fluff their wings and momentarily retreat. 'City birds,' he said. 'Take, take, take.'

The rain rang on the pavement. Wax went through his pockets. A few coins had survived the day. He counted them. There was enough for a new plan of action. First he would buy the local tabloid. Then over to the department store to try out a few Walkmans and get some change for the phonebox. It was bound to clear up before too long.

.

Philip McCann

Since graduating recently from Trinity College,
Dublin, Philip McCann has directed and written
for the professional theatre. This is his first
published work.

Grey Area

Yes, there was colour in our childhood: one autumn evening a delinquent wee splash. Generally, though, I remember it as grey: teacher's grey, a darkness in the classroom inkier even than the blackboard; crowds of blazers of a notorious charcoal that kept our identity uniformly grey; smoke-greyness of burning bus; these shades were inhaled, they went in at the eye, these dullnesses were the hue of most days. Ah, Belfast! Nowhere better to enjoy a for-old-time's-sake reminiscent puke at the past. It comes back to me in its livid tint: the odour of anthracite, Lego on the tarmac, homeless mattresses; a bombed-out sweet shop and an expedition for charred mojos; Hallion at the off-licence corner, the gangster of our street whose appearance terrified me over the years shaven head, DMs and shrunk denims revealing panic-inspiring black sock. And I remember a stock phrase of ours, very evocative of the monotone past: 'There's nothin' to do'. Another one was, 'Might as well' which represented, in the stark absence of every pastime, acquiesence to any-thing at all. Or almost anything – that wasn't taboo. And that, I suppose, is how, at the age of fourteen or so, three of us from the local Catholic 'crap school' accepted with a blasé shoulder-shrug that we *might as well* commit mur-der. Here was the dash of colour we enjoyed; but I feel it will need to be supplemented to save the reader from a similar desperation.

The rain fell. The depressed sun had slept in. Up alley and round footpath we plodded. Somehow the school drew us. Every morning there would be this wet exodus past puddles of concrete sky, oil patches, tri-coloured kerb stones; we assumed right of way through the back gardens of house-bound widows. We were all dressed the same, but we recognized each other from the back by shape and size or by the slogans on our canvas bags, all vicious but every one original. And gender also distinguished us to a certain degree from girls.

Sometimes we spotted them from the main road distantly, a sluggish cortège towards some mysterious region down the road. I would stand gazing. The morning mist became them. Far down and round the silky and moist curves of the cemetery wall there was something going on, I thought, like ad-venture or sex; something I couldn't name, but I knew it was colourful. For these girls' uniforms (if they were in fact female and therefore something diffe-rent and a kink in the smoky atmosphere) were distinctly greenish. A dull green, it is true. One might say a grey-green, a green as near to greenlessness and black while still maintaining some hope of green, but, nonetheless, a lightness sufficient to glamorize swaying haunches and swinging pigtails. I have to say 'glamorize', because girls in their plain state were not wholly unknown to us. They played round the backs in denim suits, they lived vaguely across the street or next door to someone unimportant. But in this regalia of skimpy skirts, wayward womanliness zipped into a schoolgirl's size ten, bare legs and ankle socks, never before had girls been noticed. Were they so different in truth, or was this a trick of the treacherous light? Girls, as far as I knew them, stood as men beside us boys. It was their toughness that we wished to emulate. Karen Burns, to name only one, once beat up my best friend's dad. They were physically intense like butchers or pylons, and even I, who reckoned myself fallen into cynicism deeper than most, was shocked by the distortions which they could pronounce. Now, and every morning on my protracted trudge to school, at those reluctant images of grace a new unformed knowledge stirred of tenderness somewhere.

I would arrive inside our school building, as a matter of course, after the bell, and this earned me the reputation of 'Dozeball' and the right to boast of the most dislocated ears. It was no small wonder thoughts of murder came to us so young. Some bureau-loving midnight malefactor was no doubt the cause of our first period of PE Tuesdays and Thursdays, which meant at nine o'clock a traipse out of the rain into a pair of boxer shorts and out into the rain again for a husky relay race round our blasted track. I resented with all imaginable violence and darkness the humiliation of PE and those responsible for it. It was a 9am orgy of boysweat and pimply bottoms. And the insistence afterwards that we all shamble in the nude through a cramped showering area like cattle being doused – what can I say? Fart and splash and shiver, leaking on Podge and not a flaccid member in the changing room. (Even Podge's button hardened to a piece of clove rock).And it was straight after this intimate strangeness that we were into double Latin second and third.

All the rancour I felt at that systematic stripping away of our dignity I carried into The Embryo (Mr Dornan, Latin teacher, so-called because of his formidable age, ie: he was so old he *looked* like an embryo!)

'Oh, McGuire-us! Wretche maxime!' The class sniggered wetly.

'Cordelia . . .*will* think, sir?' I ventured. He fluttered his watery eyes. '*Did* think?' Tendons appeared on his lean throat as he cleared it.

'McGuire-us, having been caught for disloyalty to the state, shall instantly be sacrificed.' His voice shook. I gazed through the page. 'McGuire-us, altar now!' I raised myself up and planted awkward steps through the schoolbags to the front of the class. 'When are you likely to learn, small boy,' he said, his fine white eyebrows trembling above me, 'that Latin is not random like your mind? We have rules, McGuire-us, logical and predictable rules, boy.' He was working himself into a passion. The parts of his body wobbled. Everybody was listening to hear what the logical consequence would be. 'McGuire-us - bucket!' The class produced a noise close to a honk. So, I took stock, it was the head-in-the-bucket routine, very predictable. I advanced to the waste-paper bin and knelt on one knee. He looked expectant.

'All the way in, sir?'

'Utmost speed, McGuire-us.' I lowered my head into the bin to the applause of my peers. Banana skin, crisp packet, Fanta tin and a nostril-crumpling whiff was the godforsaken world into which I now descended. I cursed him darkly: *One day, Embryo! I'll pickle your swollen head, have you aborted, get you fixed, etc.* At length, 'McGuire-us, sit!' was announced and, retrieving my head from the rubbish, I clodhopped back to my seat and the luxury of fresh classroom sweat. 'So fell a consequence will attend him who neglects his homework,' the thin voice quavered. 'Grogan-us, next!'

'I haven't done it either, sir.'

'Grogan-us-bucket!'

Five days a week our ignorance of the Latin language was held up to ridicule. Dido upon her pyre did not know a more nefarious sacrifice, I reckoned – except that I failed to work up ever an identification with any of that lot in togas (Virgil included) who sat about something called an arborium begging the pedagogus to teach them arithmetic on stones. The ageless Embryo and his memories of an Italy before Christ were rather removed from 'Up the Ra' and 'I'll get you tarred and feathered, wee lad, right?' I was just making this very point to Grogies one lunchtime when Vomit, the third permanent idler in Latin, so-called because his name was Vernon and his face suggestive of puke, came up to us. He had a proposition to make.

'Get him seen to.' We were roaming the football pitch, an isolated part of the school grounds we often had to ourselves. 'Muldoon has this phone number.' Grogies polished off a bottle of coke and gave it an underhand flick onto the grass bank.

'What're you talkin' about?' Grogies was half Vomit's size, his head and figure having been squashed at some stage from above. He peered up fatly as Vomit spoke.

'You know the way The Embryo's really into the IRA and all?'

'Is he?' I asked.

'Yeah?' Grogies hurried him, ignoring me.

'Well, look, Muldoon has this number.'

They were thinking too fast for me. 'What number?'

'Brilliant,' said Grogies.

'Fool-proof,' said Vomit.

'Is he really into the IRA and all?' I still wanted to know. Down at the school building we heard the bell, as impatient and periphrastic as The Embyro himself.

'How did Muldoon get the number?' Grogies now asked.

'Is he really for the IRA?'

'No, it doesn't matter. I don't know where he got it from,' Vomit said to the both of us. 'C'mon, or he'll start into us.' We shuffled down the steps from the pitch to the playground and along to the school building, hastening slowly to a double bill of mythology.

For the rest of the day that conversation preoccupied me. Weren't they urging, though I could barely bring myself to acknowledge it, the real live death of The Embryo? By some intricate deceit involving telephone calls? Murder most foul! As the days crawled by and lunchtimes were taken up with resentment, details began to slot together in a water-tight plan of revenge. It was a fantasy, of course, the whole time. It did not even gain credence as a moment of delusion. We had never been serious, though we planned it right up to the synchronization of watches. Still, strangely enough, we goaded each other on, producing ever finer details, choosing the best day to strike. I only swore in dead earnest to perplex Puke-face and Action Man Grogan. To actually *do* it would have been a brand new concept entirely. And so, with the passing of weeks, once our plan had been perfected, there was a silent agreement to drop it. Latin was endured.

But, then, one Thursday at break Grogies came up to me by the lockers.

'I wanna kill The Embyro,' he hissed. We had just enjoyed his public humiliation for confusing *unless* and *therefore*.

'Do you?' I said.

'Yeah.' Our looks were pregnant. That lunchtime the three of us arranged to meet after school to discuss the alternatives to stoicism.

A handy converging point for each of us was the half-lamppost at McPeake's sweetshop. In addition to being halved, it was a lamppost which small boys made consistent efforts to ignite. I arrived early, so I propped half a buttock on a low wall and stared across the road at Robinson's house. It was painted blue. For some reason that annoyed me. There was something conspicuously employed about having a blue house. It was conspicuously un-green, un-Irish, but that wasn't what annoyed me. It was simply the blueness I objected to, or the prettiness. I contemplated a graffiti job during the night, or a soundless arcing of eggs from out of the evening. The liberal side to having no law and order was that ideas could ramify. The confidential phone number was an inspiration of its own. Maybe we could ring up the Brits, I thought, and say Mr Robinson was an activist. In turn Mr Robinson might ring up Sinn Fein and implicate everyone's choice, the obvious Hallion deliciously in a scandal of treachery. It was marvellously liberating, this underhand tipping off with fictions. Morally, it seemed sound enough, especially if it could ever get Hallion insidiously done in.

My thoughts were distracted by two outlines: one disproportionately stretched and one disproportionately stumpy schoolboy.

'Hiya.'

'Hiya.'

'Well?'

'Well?' Vomit leaned against the midget lamppost. A low sky raced above our heads.

'Will we do it?'

'I don't know. Do you want to?' A car skidded by.

'We get the number of the UDA off Muldoon, right?' A bottle smashed.

'Is Muldoon a prod?'

'Don't be stupid!'

'Ring up on Saturday morning, right? Say Dornan's in the IRA, has all these guns and all.'

'Do you want to?'

'Suppose so.' A soldier ran past us watchfully, followed by another, then another.

'Write it out on a bit of paper. One of us'll read it out.'

'In a different accent.'

'Yeah.'

'Will we?'

'Why not?'

'What else is there to do?'

Some sort of riot on the road seemed imminent. We decided to shift. 'Let's go to our house,' Grogies suggested. He, having come across sea-sickness tablets in the medicine cabinet in his house and having noted that they contained codeine, now proposed that we try to get high in celebration of our brand new concept. So off we went to his bald bedroom to go over the details again and eat Quells. Not surprisingly, it was an evening of 'I think I can feel something', 'Can you?', 'Maybe not', and much time devoted to worrying about the perils of overdosing on four tablets. Grogan tried to retch in a panic at the last moment and couldn't, while I sat on the bed awaiting the arrival of sensation: a patient and sober wait ending in self-contempt. My image of us as fated to a life of vice and self-abandon was not sustaining. But the evening was far from compos mentis. We fixed a time and a place to begin the execution of our plot: ten o'clock, Saturday, my house.

Using a domestic phone for our purposes would have been simply unwise, we concurred, (possibility of tracing, tapping, bugging) so, nearer to noon than ten on the chosen day, we set out from my front door with our secret number and our message towards the closest kiosk. There was, as we knew, a bombed-out shell at the bottom of my narrow terraced street, container of human excrement and contraceptives, its royal red slopped over with green (for Eire) and concluded with a paint bomb (to scarlet). Turning in the opposite direction, we walked to the top of the street and onto the main road. There was an amplified voice from somewhere, tinny, unintelligible.

'Well, where will we find one?' Vomit said. As he scanned, realization dawned on his face. It dawned on me too: were we searching for a telephone in our area *in working order*? Even the footpaths here were broken! Expecting there to be a telephone struck me suddenly as subversive. Across the road from us now we could see a woman shouting into a microphone in front of a row of shops. A handful of people had gathered. She could have been yelling at us for not smashing up the shops or wrecking someone's car. I peered nervously down the road in the direction of the cemetery.

'Down there,' I said. Occasionally a car would sound its horn on the way past the loud voice. None of us had ever been down there. 'Down there,' I repeated. In shame I was concealing from them my absurd hope that we would come across gentle girls in green uniforms on their way from school (even though this was Saturday) or just naturally staying (because this was girl country, a coloured place). 'Right,' said Grogies, and, with a strong faith that down there solution lay, we set off towards the cemetery.

The clouds were splashed with muddy water. Vomit chatted to himself: 'This is mad,' and, 'This'll teach him a lesson.' As we skirted the cemetery, golden clouds passed between the chimneys of an old factory. There were little cloths drooping from the lampposts. I remembered them being strung up the summer before as mourning flags in defiance for the hunger strikers. By now the rain had washed them white. The traffic was pulling out round a burning car. There weren't any kiosks about. Eventually I said, 'This is useless.'

'Is that a phone box?' Grogies spoke over my words. It was difficult to say if it was or not. A whitish reddish daub on the far footpath did almost resemble in shape at least one side of a kiosk. And, in effect, that is what it proved to be: a solitary door to nowhere standing clean in a concrete base, one part red, nine parts white. I gave an exasperated smack through my lips.

'This is fuckin' stupid.'

'Let's get off this crappy road,' Grogies said, so at the next turning on the right we diverted our course down a tree-lined road.

'Let's go over it all again,' said Vomit, being mature. I felt a spit of rain.

'I ring up,' Grogies sighed with a dubious glance at me.

'Remember the accent.'

'And what do you say?'

'It's written down!'

'What do you say anyway?' We broke into a children's game of football. Somewhere a fire was burning.

'Eddie Dornan of whatever the street is . . . has a garden of IRA arms. . . . Em . . .'

'If you . . .' Vomit prompted.

'Oh aye, if you don't get rid of him fast, we will.'

'Remember the accent,' I said.

'All right!' he flared up. We came to a busy roundabout. Separately, we dashed through the traffic to the far footpath. When Grogies made it across, bouncing up to us on his short legs, we resumed.

'And then you hang up.'

'Mm.'

'Brilliant.'

'Do you think he'll get shot?'

'Hope so.'

'Knee-capped anyway.'

I tutted. 'Jammy bastard!'

We joined another road off the roundabout. There were some soldiers laughing up ahead. Together they formed a shrub of camouflage that broke the monotony of paving.

'Where're we goin'?' Vomit dropped his voice. But before he could get an answer, and rather more swiftly than I can recount here, we were spread-eagled against one side of a jeep. Normally this was a safe enough routine provided you were polite. But Grogies was *too* polite. They wanted us to empty out our pockets. Everything went onto the bonnet of the jeep: handkerchief, chewed biro top, locker keys, balls of fluff and that slip of paper Grogies was going to read from. My heart started to thud. If they read that, my mind was racing, we won't just be lifted. It'll be bloody internment maybe! As we were being frisked I kept my eyes on it, sitting apart from the other things, folded in a half-open inviting V. A soldier poked through everything. It was unmistakably eye-catching, I thought, a note, it was obvious he would read it.

'Turn round,' he said. 'What's this?' His English accent pierced the clotted light. Standing to face him, I then knew myself to be a cloud of vagueness which his voice now dispersed, pinning us to facts which I had been perfectly happy to fudge or blur. That slip of paper was a death sentence, or if it wasn't, that's what we wanted it to be. There would be no smudging the fat edge between right and wrong with these boys. This was attempted murder, there was no neutral zone set aside for mitigating circumstances. 'What's this?' he repeated. I sickened. I saw my father's face suddenly involved, and me all tears blubbering, 'We didn't mean it.' How had this all happened in a moment, I puzzled, a stern soldier with an RAF moustache being literal about a blur and a

Philip McCann

daydream. 'They're car keys!' the soldier spoke again. He was holding up our locker keys.

'They're our locker keys,' Vomit was saying. My heart was boxing on the wall of my chest. 'They're locker keys.'

'What you doing round 'ere? You're doing cars, ain't ya?'

'They're locker keys,' Vomit tried to explain. 'We've lockers in school. They're locker keys.'

'I'll put you inside that fucking jeep in a minute.' Vomit was silenced. 'Where d'you live?'

'Twenty-seven . . .' That note was shifting in the breeze. The soldier behind began singing our addresses into a walkie-talkie.

'What you doing round 'ere, then? You shouldn't be outside your area.'

'We're goin' for a walk,' Grogies volunteered.

'Doing what?' He wrung his face for some fierce disbelief. True enough, it did seem somewhat eccentric to be strolling off the beaten track into a wilderness like here, wherever we were. The soldier with the walkie-talkie got some reply.

'Okay, take your things,' the one with the moustache said. We clutched for everything. 'You shouldn't be out of your area,' he bawled, climbing into the jeep.

We plonked self-consciously away, feeling muzzles with eyes on the backs of our necks. I was still nervous. There wasn't much tenderness round here, I thought bitterly. This area was alarmingly short of young females to run up and comfort us. We came into the centre of the city soon. We didn't feel like talking. We found a vinegary hamburger joint.

'What did he want to know all that for, anyway?' Vomit and Grogan began to chat round our table. But something else had stung me. We weren't in a position to be righteous, but all the same . . . What did he mean we shouldn't be out of our area? What would keep us there, except Quells and cough bottles on Saturday evenings? The both of them munched away. I didn't order. I just sat looking out at two policemen with their bullet-proof vests and rubber bullet guns. It would be dark soon. There were no shoppers passing on the street. It was peaceful except for, somewhere, the clicking of a metal turnstile. Eventually Grogan said, 'What'll we do?' I stared out of the window instead of answering. A dog trotted past the two policemen. It began to drizzle. After a bit I stopped looking out of the window.

'This is crap, isn't it?' I said. Grogan looked at me with long stupid eyelashes.

'Yeah,' he said.

We sat until the shower eased off, then we got up. We stepped out into the early evening without talking. We simply walked round to get a black taxi up the road. Before we got there we passed a market stall. Beside it there was a telephone kiosk. We stopped.

'Is there any point seein' if it works?'

'Not really,' said Vomit. He tried it anyway. 'It's workin',' he said.

'Well?'

'Well?' said Grogan.

A new excitement started to cheer me up. I shrivelled like The Embryo. 'Therefore?' I crooned. 'What can we conclude?'

'It's fuckin' not sensible anyway!' laughed Grogan.

'Let's do it,' I said.

'The whole thing's crazy,' said Vomit with all the Apollonian dryness he could muster to counter my impulse.

'C'mon!' I urged them, grinning. I opened the door with my weight.

'What do *you* think?' Vomit asked. Grogies thought for a moment.

'It's murder,' he said.

'So fuck!' I said loudly. He looked at Vomit.

'Might as well,' he said.

'We might as well,' I repeated.

We all got into the kiosk. Grogies ferreted for the slip of paper. There was a piece of one of the windows lying on the shelf inside like a big set square.

'What's the number?' We laughed. I dialled it as Grogies clutched the receiver, listening intently. We all heard the ringing tone. It kept ringing. Suddenly he slammed his hand on the rest. We giggled together. 'I'm not ready.' I started to dial again. 'No, I wanna rehearse,' he said.

I squeezed round to look through the misted glass. On a cloud was a sticker of the moon, torn in half. The army drove past. 'Look,' I said, 'do it and we'll get out of here.' I angled the slip of paper in Grogies' hand towards me and dialled the number again.

'Jesus!' He crossed his legs. We heard the ringing tone again. It rang and rang. And then, strangely, Grogies turned away from us and was fully into his act, a finger in his ear, frowning.

The next moment he hauled an arm up through the squash of our bodies and, with a karate chop, cut himself off. He looked at us, exhausted, expectant. We looked back at him, so he said, 'It was a woman answered.' We didn't say anything for a moment. Then Vomit mumbled, 'We've actually done it.'

'I know,' I said.

'We shouldn't have. It was really banal.' We looked at each other.

'I know,' said Grogan.

On the way round to the black taxis and in the queue we didn't speak. When our turn came we squeezed in with three woman who nattered all the way up the road. Until we got out of the taxi to part at the corner we hadn't exchanged a word since the kiosk. 'See you,' I said, breaking the silence.

'See you.'

We made off in different directions. Well, it was pretty selfish, I admitted to myself on the walk to my street – but so what? So what if it was banal? It was no more banal than this dark trek over broken glass. The whole condition was banal and that was part of it. Hallion and two others were lolling against our wall. Who gave a damn anyway? The whole long day lay behind me like my disgrace. But at least now we had acted. We did something which was more than our vague patient morose wait to be older before we'd start living. For the first time, probably, we were ourselves, unwise and ungentle. I would stew in selfishness and banality and badness before I'd let a scruple stop me from kicking out for a moment. At anything. That unloved skimpy excuse for a man, our teacher, he didn't spare a blind fuck for our pains and fears. So what if we punctured the fatuous hot air out of his one clapped-out lung? I could see him wheeze as the gunshot reverberated, a trickle of blood down his quivering chin, his spindle legs would buckle and he'd be down, red eyes blinking for mercy. Beautiful!

Andrew Miller

Born in Bristol in 1960, Andrew Miller studied in
Middlesex, then lived and taught abroad before
coming to Norwich. He was the winner of the
Arvon Writers Short Story Competition in 1987.
The Sweet and the Vile is his latest work.

The Sweet and the Vile

This fridge, in case you were wondering, we got at Donny's in the new year sales. A Huelomatic-Supra with a three year guarantee and, lucky for me, an ice making capacity in advance of any comparable machine on the market today. It was Donny's Machine of the Month. A massive leap forward in refrigeration technology. But what really tipped the balance is that for every fridge bought cash down Mr Donny, who happens to be president of the Snuffdon-Anchorage link, sends a fiver to an orphaned Eskimo kid. Beautiful little things. It's a lonely old game though, waiting for water to freeze. By rights I should be tucked up in the Dreamaster instead of sitting here staring at the fridge door gasping on my sixtieth Superking. We'll all know who's to blame when I go down with the big C. In fact you could say it's been one of those weeks, though I think both of us have grown incredibly as people. Me more than her of course, that's to be expected. I just don't want you thinking it's all been a walk in the park. Fortunately the colour scheme in here is incredibly restful.

See those cupboards? I put them up. You get them in kit form from Donny's with a choice of four great shades: Autumn Gooseberry, Ambrosia, Wild Elm and Arctic Blue. Usual story. She wanted Ambrosia and I wanted Arctic Blue. Thing is, she went on and on about it until Muggins here had to nip her in the ankle with the shopping trolley. They're a bloody disgrace those trolleys, war chariots. You'd think I'd shot her in the leg with a dumdum bullet. I had to stuff her in the trolley all arse about tit, bleeding over the frozen burgers and the disinfectant and wheel her to the Hypermarket Medi-Centre. 'Do you possess a Donnycard Sir?' Too right I do. Anyway they patched her up, a lovely job. Scarless. A little fire-cracker of a nurse in a stripey green dress and a straw hat. And this young trainee-manager with eczema, who was learning the ropes. I said, 'Here mate, get the missus a Babycham,' and tried to push a fiver in his back pocket but, 'No, no sir, it's all part of The Highway to Health Complete Family Care Deal Modern Medicine at a Price You Can Afford.'

The lad with eczema gave me a booklet. A beautiful glossy thing with a great full colour snap inside of the Donny family having a caper in the countryside. I wouldn't care to say how often I've read it. It bucks you up. They've even – I remember waking her up that night to tell her – got their own Chapel of Rest smack between the Senior Citizens' Muster point and the wet fish stall ('Is it fresh or is it *Donny* fresh?'). Mind you, we didn't go out much. When you've got a nice home you don't need to. Next door used to pop round, he's in pensions, ex-SAS or something but I didn't encourage it. I'd just sit there and stare at the carpet until they left. Soft bastards sent the wife a leaflet about mental health provision, but it did the trick. In my book when you tie the knot that's it. There's no cause to go yakking with strangers. Anyway, Mrs Brain of Britain says, 'What about you, spending half your life in The Crown?' 'Why,' I said, 'does everything have to be explained? Haven't I got enough on my plate? Your problem is that you don't know how special you are. I turn you over like a coin in my pocket all day.' 'So,' she says, pouring a whack of Mirage into her coffee, 'that's where I am is it?' That was our little joke. We should have had another really, it would have eased the tension. I'm a great believer in jokes. Laughter is the sunshine of life and we all need a bit of sunshine. I don't care who you are. Ice is ready. Up we go.

I like that sound. Ice falling. I don't know what it sounds like except ice but it makes me think of those ads. You know, the one where they're on the train and the geezer in the white jacket drops the ice in their glasses and pours the stuff in and they grin at each other and the train goes into a tunnel. No prizes for guessing the smooth bastard and the old geezer are giving her one in the tunnel. Beautiful. But what I like, what I really like, is cosiness. It sounds soft, but those bits when it was just the two of us and the Coalite, they're all in here like a row of incredibly bright Polaroid photos. Me and her on the sofa pecking at something on toast and watching one of those nature programmes on the box. Now and then I'd squeeze her hand just to let her know I was there and see how long she could stand it. Do you ever get a stiffy watching those nature programmes? Works for me every time. Unbelievably sordid the way fish carry on, and the insects are even worse. I sometimes get the feeling that everything in Nature is either puking or bonking. Dogs are all right, they'll attack who you tell them to. And horses. The way they thunder about, licking themselves and trampling on people, incredible. There's this pratt used to drink at the Crown who did it with bread. Now if he doesn't have a Hovis first thing he feels wrong all day. You won't catch a horse doing that. Mind you, women like it too, all bloody ways, Jesus Christ! You should have seen her in the beginning. Talk about on heat! Luckily I'm not exactly under-endowed. Bigger than Geoff anyway. We'd have a sex romp over that sink sometimes, when she was doing the dinner things. You've got to treasure the memories, eh?

While we're at it I'll tell you what else I like. Tracksuits. Really unbelievably comfortable things. Here's my idea of heaven. A cold can of Carling, big bag of scratchings, and me and my princess on the sofa in tracksuits watching Life on Earth (the one with the bonking scorpions). I made sure of course her tracky was the same as mine, City Stripe. I liked us looking alike, it was tidy and made her easier to find, particularly on a Saturday morning at Donny's. That was the high point of our week. Get up nice and early, a quick gargle with the old anti-plaque, a couple of Superkings then bundle into the Caprice and burn a hole through the dozy bastards on the bypass. Down at Donny's I'd park up and give her a soppy little bite just by her eye. I can remember her saying, 'You funny old thing', but she never said it in fact: she was too busy slapping the window to get help. Nobody ever came, though. That's what I love about this country. That and the moment when those big glass doors swish open and a voice from above says 'Welcome' and tells you what the special offers are. Then you pick up a trolley and start off down those tall shining aisles. You'll laugh but it made me feel like we were getting married all over again. Whole walls of toilet paper from cream to crimson. Over forty different brands of dog food. Two hundred varieties of lager. Satellite dishes that look like sun umbrellas. Go-fast stripes and chromium hubs for the motor, insect repellent and astroturf for the garden. Crinkly shrink-wrapped packs of rubber gloves and briefcases. Half the veg I'd never even heard of. Things that looked like tomatoes but were green inside and tasted of strawberries, potatoes that you peeled and ate like a banana. I mean, where else can you get a three-piece suit, a bowie knife and a whole pig in aspic under the same roof? When we'd done we'd nip upstairs to the Happy Flipper fish bar for a bit of a blow out. You could tell how much she liked it. I remember her smiling once when she got a bone in her throat. 'My plucky girl,' I said, 'you're too good for me. A princess in a tracksuit. A bloody marvel.'

But have you noticed how people change? They learn a new word and then they can't stop using it. Who'd have thought a word could make so much difference? Hers was 'no'. Christ knows where she picked that up. Probably from that bitch with a face like a bag of nails who used to sit around here with her gob glued to the side of a coffee cup. Rolling her own fags. I ask you. What did they talk about ? 'Just things,' she said. 'What kind of things?' 'Just things,' like a bloody parrot. I start seeing red of course and next thing her hand is in the drawer. Still, she stuck to our little agreement about no screaming in the house. I respected her for that because the neighbours are great whisperers. You see, she was loyal in her way, a funny old way of showing it sometimes but she could see, you see.

I've got feelings too. A forinstance: some of us lads at The Crown started a fund for this cripple kid to go to Czechoslovakia. We've got a nice colour snap of the little mite grinning with all her crutches and stuff. I'm vice-captain of the sponsored pool team playing The Eagle next Wednesday. Melanie, the kid's called. Great big eyes like a puppy and a red bow in her hair. In fact I wouldn't mind popping round and seeing Melanie, gee her up a bit, take her out for a run in the Caprice. You should have heard Geoff going on about her.

You'd like Geoff. Geoffy. He's quiet but a thinker. You know what they say about still dark horses running deep. Doesn't matter what the weather, Geoff's up at the bar in his running shorts, those silky looking jobs split at the sides and Nike trainers. Funny really because he can hardly walk. Got legs like a corpse. Geoff of course is captain of the pool team. He's always doing things for kids. Some of us even thought of nominating him for one of those shows where the wall turns round and you're in a TV studio and Esther what's-her-face is running towards you with a huge purple heart and everyone you've ever known is clapping and crying. 'The other night,' he said, 'I said a prayer for that little girl, and I haven't been on my knees since my old mum went off.' Kids, they're like flowers, some grow up straight and bloom with incredible colours but the others fall on stony ground or some pervert comes along. A complete bloody tragedy. Then this geezer Tony who once had an epileptic fit in the lounge bar says, 'Have you ever thought of social work?' 'As a matter of fact,' says Geoff and this Tony laughs in his face. 'You ought to be gassed,' says Geoff. Anyway, I told Geoff what she'd been asking for, clothes and things and a lock on the bathroom door and he says, 'Old son, give her the night of her life. The works, the whole bloody caboodle'. Well, that's what I did. This ice takes an age.

Anyway. I booked us in at Don Benito's and told Mrs Benito that when I scratched myself that was the signal to bring on a couple of Don Benito's Emperors' choice ice-cream bombs with sparklers. My little girl hadn't been eating for the last week, so for starters I ordered her one of those eighteen-inch deep-pan jobs loaded with pineapple and anchovy and a couple of fried eggs. Well she just sat and stared at it like her brain had gone so I cut it up and forked it into her gob, though most of it ended up on her dress. I'll tell you what though, she looked the business. I can't say what it was exactly but, even unconscious, she had this sort of elegance. I suppose that's what drew me to her. 'You know who we are?' I said. 'Torvill and Dean.' That cheered her up and I let her have one of my Superkings though as a rule I don't like her to smoke in public. Anyway, what with one thing leading to another, the music and the candlelight, pretty soon I'm having a little paddle in her minge and it's just getting interesting when Mrs Benito, thinking its the sign, breezes up with the sparklers and ice-cream. Well, the old slag nearly has a double haemorrhage and runs around the restaurant screaming at the top of her lungs in Italian. And they say Eyeties are romantic.

Well, we had to leave of course, and to cap it all, guess who does a Hughie Green on the way home, anchovies and fried egg all down the side of the Caprice! I'd only waxed it on the Sunday so you'd have thought she'd want to make amends when we got in, but no, not Madame. 'Have a look at this,' I said and showed her the bill. 'Don't know the meaning of the word gratitude do we?' Well, we had a bit of a rough house and I locked her in the garage for the night.

I'm not proud of that. Breaks my heart when I think of her little face and that sexy black number of hers all covered in puke and pizza. Right, I thought, we'll make a fresh start, so next morning I had a nice hot bath and took her some tea in the garage. She didn't look too bad, a bit on the vacant side but I was ready for that. I got a couple of videos in and we settled down on the sofa, just the two of us, incredibly snug. I had my Carlings and scratchings and she had a bottle of that Mirage crap and a box of capsules. Christ knows how many she took. After about an hour she fell into my lap, good as gold. I just stroked and stroked her hair and whispered, you know, daft things: 'You're the only girl for me', 'Sweet dreams my precious, my lamb'. Her skin was soft as new gloves. About lunchtime I touched her bottom lip with a ciggy just to make sure. Nothing. Well, I thought, she didn't suffer. That's the main thing. Slipped away.

Still, it pulls on the old heart strings something like that and I was having a bit of a blub when suddenly I thought, Hang on a mo, she's probably somewhere with Geoff's mum having a natter. That pulled me round. I propped her up on a bean bag and slipped down The Crown for a couple. I didn't feel too bad considering. Every rainbow has a silver lining and, looked at in the right way, her crossing over could help to bring us closer, make us more of a team. A chance to get to know each other again. I'll tell you this, if you don't take the time to work on a relationship one day you'll find yourself living with a stranger.

I knew of course Saturdays at Donny's were going to be different but, really it was just a matter of adapting. I took the rest of the week off so we could make the most of things. A couple of nights ago I even took her out in the Caprice, a beautiful moonlit night. I expect you can guess where we went. Unfortunately, just as I was thinking of having a quick cuddle, a security van shows up. I'd forgotten about the infra-red cameras. In fact it gave me a bit of a turn, but you'd have laughed out loud if you'd seen how calm she looked, sat there with a strange little smile on her face. Anyway, it was when I was carrying her back into the house that I noticed something was up. At first I thought I'd left some bacon out and then it dawned on me. She's going manky. Well, no one likes to think of a loved one going past their sell-by date like that and I was on the verge of asking Geoff or that nurse at Donny's what I ought to do, when out of the blue the word Huelomatic pops into my mind. Right mate. So I carried her up to the bathroom, cut her togs off with the kitchen scissors, slipped her into the tub and started filling it up with ice. It's ironic really because she always said she felt the cold, that it crept into her bones, poor love, and something about the thinness of her blood. Well, she was the nervy sort, dive out of her skin if someone screamed or if I took a corner blindly in the Caprice. That was what attracted me, her being so emotional. Just snap your fingers in her face and off she'd run for one of those capsules and a dry little blub in the kazi. I'll tell you what though, it's brought her complexion back. We had a laugh about that earlier on. Looking more composed, I said and she made a sort of gassy sound.

Of course our relationship is more spiritual now. Quite frankly I've lost the urge as far as she's concerned. I'll have a little grieve then pop along to Donny's for a chat with that eczema lad and see if we can't sort something. You'll think I'm daft but I've got this dream, a beautiful little thing like a cherry drop in the middle of my brain. We're all gathered round the coffin in the Chapel of Rest. Me, Geoff, and little Melanie strapped to her chair when, out of the blue there's this noise like new leather at the back and who should be coming forward extending his sympathies but Mr D. He has a few quiet words with me about how sorry he is to lose such a good customer and something about a memorial trolley and then pats my arm and slow marches to the furnace door. Bundles her in in person. Then the little Donnys come in holding candles and read poems they've written at school about looking on the bright side and having a wheeze. I, of course, lose control completely and have to be sedated. That nurse in the straw hat's giving me the kiss of life and Mr D's offering his bone marrow and all sorts. Even Esther what's-her-face is there, completely moved. Next thing I know we're in The Crown putting it all behind us. Geoff's singing *Abide with me* and Carling's half-price all night. 'Get stuck in, lads,' says Mr D, then with his own gold pen writes out a cheque for the whole bloody bunch of us to go to Czechoslovakia. Typical.

Anyway, that's my dream. It's probably Geoff's dream too. As for her, well I don't think she ever had any dreams. I never encouraged them. I could tell you other things, funny things about me and her, the stuff we got up to, but I've put you in the picture now and it doesn't do to live in the past. All water under the belt, as a wise man once put it. No point crying over sleeping dogs. So that's about it then.

Bugger off.

Nairne Plouviez

In her early twenties Nairne Plouviez was married and settled
down in London to have children. She worked for a literary
agency before training as a teacher. While teaching in
Hackney, she studied for a degree from Birkbeck College. She
lives and writes in Norwich.

Bees

The fine dust rose and fell, gently mottling the stainless steel sink and Driscoll wondered why it was his father couldn't make toast. 'A bit burnt. Sorry.' He took the toast and spread butter over it thickly. 'Now what?' His father looked around the kitchen as if trying to remember something. 'Money.' He put a pile of coins on the table in front of Driscoll. 'Take what you need for playcentre. Got your key? Straight home, no loitering.'

Driscoll nodded. The key felt cold and hard against his skin. He took two pounds from the pile of coins and put them in his pocket. He noticed a smudge of oil from his bicycle chain on his hand. He pushed back his fringe which had grown so long it tickled his eyelids and remembered he hadn't brushed his teeth. 'Can I take some pie for Jason? His Aunt's not half stingy with the food.' He didn't like lying to his father. 'Go ahead. There's some pie in the fridge, I think.' He wrapped the pie in a piece of kitchen towel and put it in his school bag. 'Still bees, is it?' his father asked. 'Hope they'll teach you something useful. I suppose we've gotta wait till next year for the comprehensive, have we?' Driscoll kissed his father's face with its furrows and spidery lines that criss-crossed each other like twigs and branches. There seemed to be more creases since his mother had gone.

'Kate Bayley is helping me make the hexagons for the hive,' he said. 'Then we're going to stick them together . . .' He glanced at the bundle of thick white straws that lay beside the cake tin. 'Run along, Driscoll, you'll be late.' His father opened the newspaper and disappeared behind it.

His school bag knocked against his legs and the wind hurt his face as he ran down the road into the alley and into Rory.

'Slow up lad, slow up. Give us a 'and with this lot, Driscoll.'

The remains of Rory's bed lay on the pavement, a flattened cardboard box with giant footsteps on it and some newspapers which Driscoll began to gather together. Rory produced a piece of grey string from his pocket and tied it around the papers. The khaki coat Rory wore smelt musty and there were long white hairs in his beard and eyebrows. As he stood up he looked huge and dark against the summer blue sky. 'Got me food?' Driscoll removed the pie from his bag and watched as Rory unwrapped it, smelt it, wrapped it up again and put it into one of the white plastic carrier bags that stood huddled together by the wall. 'Now a cuppa and a smoke.'

Turning up his coat collar against the wind, he put the newspapers under his arm, picked up the carriers and began walking towards the main road. Driscoll followed.

'Got any news, Rory?'

'Might 'ave, might 'ave,' he muttered and walked on. As he pushed open the café door the warm air drifted around them like scent. 'Coming in then?' Rory asked. He knew he should go to school, but the possibility of news and the girl smiling at them through steam from the urn drew him in. 'Patsy, this is the lad's lost his mother.'

The girl looked at Driscoll as she poured out two cups of tea. 'What happened, then, why'd she go off?' she asked.

'She's lost.' Driscoll noticed his voice sounded small.

'A bit of a domestic rumpus if you ask me,' Rory said as he moved to one of the tables.

'Go on, Rory, tell us, has someone seen her?'

'Lily *may* have. That was a bit faint, that photo. She's been looking out for you. Where you said, and she may 'ave seen 'er.' He blew smoke around them.

'Can we go and see? Find Lily? See if it's her? Can we? Please, Rory. Phone the school for us. I can stay all day then.'

'Let me finish my tea first.' Driscoll had learnt over the past weeks that Rory would never be hurried.

'What's a domestic rumpus?'

'Oh you know a tiff, a fall-out.'

'She might have gone 'cos of me.'

'What you done then?' Rory said as he blew smoke around them. 'Something bad, I'll be bound.'

'Dunno do I?' Driscoll could see Rory's yellow teeth as he smiled at him. Unable to restrain himself any longer, he added quietly, 'Can we go, Rory? Please? I've got two pounds for fares. I'll keep on bringing the food after, even if it's her.'

'I'm not going on no trains or buses. We'll have to walk it. And you mustn't talk all day, you're a mate now, aren't yer?'

'I won't talk, honest and I'm a good walker.'

'Right then, we will. But don't get your 'opes up, Driscoll. There's a hellava lotta people around here.'

They stood behind the counter and the receiver looked small in Rory's hand.

'. . . 'e's poorly. 'e's sicking up. We've called the doctor . . .'

Driscoll shook his sleeve. 'Say goodbye.'

Patsy winked at him: 'Bunking off, eh?'

He had been bunking off the day he had met Rory. Not that he did it all that often. A girl in his class had been to Brighton and all sorts. Next day in the playground she'd told them about the donkeys on the beach. He wouldn't do that. They all did it sometimes, got someone to write a note for Miss Trimmer. Kate's brother, who was nearly grown-up, wrote lots of notes using all different handwriting to fool her. You were considered a wally if you didn't bunk off sometimes. He had met Rory one day outside one of the big stores. He had looked so miserable standing in front of that plate-glass window with loads of stuff like videos and tellies behind him that he had given a sandwich out of his packed lunch. That was how they got friendly.

Then he used to visit him in the alley on his way to school and tell him about the bee project. Rory liked listening, said he was keen on nature. He had bunked off the day his mother had left. All his dad could do was cry and he hated seeing him cry. Driscoll kept asking, 'Where's she gone, why did she go?' And his dad said she'd gone to sort herself out, she needed time alone, she was lost. One day his father had said she was living somewhere in Bethnal Green and had got herself a job. That was when he had taken the photo out of the album and Rory had said he would put the word around his friends who lived that way. He stopped asking about her because he didn't like it when his dad cried. Taking food for Rory wasn't difficult because his dad was always tired and sort of busy in his head. But he had made up the story about Jason's aunt not giving him enough to eat so that he could take more than an apple or a slice of bread. Rory got cross if he asked too often. He used to say, 'Don't nag. Keep me fuelled and we'll see what we can do.'

The trouble with bunking off was that he missed the bee project. If he wasn't there someone might spoil the hive he was building. He was good at art and Miss Trimmer had chosen him and Kate to build it. They were making hexagons out of straws and then they would stick them together for the hive. One group was making larvae to put in some of the hexagons while the rest would be filled with cotton wool, dyed yellow to look like honey. Another group was making worker bees which would go with the flower painting because they collect the pollen. Beth Rawlings, who was the best at sewing, was making the Queen out of yellow and black felt. Then it would all be put together, the queen in the centre, the larvae and honey in their cells and the worker bees hung from the ceiling on cotton or something, flying between the flowers and the hive. It all made sense somehow, everything fitted together. It was going to be great. Trouble was, it didn't make bunking off as much fun as it might be. Still, today was different, today was important.

Leaving their bags behind the counter so they could travel light, they set off. Rory, having made sure he had his piece of pie in his pocket, led the way and Driscoll followed, dodging through the crowds behind him. Occasionally Rory slowed up and they walked beside each other in silence. They went down roads where there were hotels with exotic names like Grecian Palace and Indian children spilt onto the steps and pavement; they went across squares where large houses with gates and gardens stared vacantly at each other; along streets where the litter blew aimlessly around their feet; through estates where the blocks of flats cast long shadows, and where some boys, leaning over a balcony like gargoyles, shouted down, 'Is that your dad? Bet 'e stinks.' As they turned the corner, Driscoll turned back and stuck his tongue out at them.

They walked past houses that wore burglar alarms like badges. 'Nobs' country, this,' Rory said and, finding a stick, excavated a litter bin, adding, 'Good pickings.' As he noticed that people turned to look at Rory, struck by his ragged and fierce appearance, Driscoll decided to walk behind, not beside him. A small black boy began darting along just in front of him like a tug.

'Wanta piece of gum? What yer doing? Bunking off? I am. School's a loada rubbish.' Driscoll chewed and didn't reply. 'Like football? I'm good. Wicked. Watch.' He negotiated between two women waiting to cross the road. 'See that? Did yer? Come to the park? Go on. Do yer smoke? I do.'

'Hey!' Driscoll stopped and looked down. 'Push off. I'm busy.'

As he walked on the boy shouted after him, 'Wanker!'

They walked down a street where a Chinese take-away was squashed between two houses, and a newsagents where papers outside flapped in the wind. Driscoll stopped to watch a car pass, its occupant sitting far behind a chauffeur. As he looked back a woman ran out of a doorway followed by a man wearing braces. The woman hopped as she took off one shoe, her hair blowing across her face. She raised the shoe above her head and the man grasped her arm, twisting her wrist until the shoe fell on the pavement at Driscoll's feet. An old woman stood watching, she shook her head and said something Driscoll couldn't hear. The man and the woman swayed back and forth, glaring at each other. Then, scooping up the shoe with his free hand, the man pulled the woman towards the doorway. She limped after him. Driscoll looked up and saw Rory turn the corner. He pushed past the old woman and ran on.

Driscoll wondered whether to tell Rory what he had seen but, remembering his promise to be silent, said nothing. He was relieved when Rory stopped and said, 'Gotta have a fag.' He sank down onto the pavement, his back against a low wall, and the green coat lay heavily around him on the grey stone. 'Sit down, Driscoll.' Driscoll squatted beside him. He pulled his jacket around him, crossed his arms and tucked his cold hands under his armpits. Small white clouds slid across the sky. Two women walked past and peered down at them like herons. By the way their heads moved towards each other Driscoll thought they were talking about them. Wisps of smoke drifted towards the trees which stood regimentally along the narrow road. Rory flicked his cigarette end into the road and got up. Dust rose from his coat and a few pieces of paper clung to its fibres.

As they passed a school playground, Driscoll stopped to watch the children, realizing it must be eleven o'clock. He watched the boy in goal and wondered who would be in goal at school today. Ben always wanted to be but since he had let in two goals, which had led to a fight in the classroom, they probably wouldn't let him. A girl came up and stood looking at him, her face patchy where the sun cast shadows through the coarse mesh fence.

'What's your name?' she asked.

'Driscoll,' he answered still watching the match.

'Where you going?'

'Somewhere.' He watched as a boy with red hair kicked the ball between two piles of sweaters that marked out the goal mouth. 'Who's that?' He nodded towards the boy.

'Gary. He's in Miss French's class.' A girl, her arms around a yellow plastic ball, came up. 'Guess what?' The first girl turned to her friend. 'His name's Driscoll.' They started to giggle together.

Driscoll followed the ball as it was passed from one player to another. Who would he have in his team? He wished he could join in. As the whistle blew and the children froze, waiting to be called in class by class, he looked along the road and realized that Rory wasn't in sight.

'I've gotta go. Bye,' he shouted to the girls, whose fingers wriggled through the mesh at him.

Driscoll knew that Rory, who moved slowly, wouldn't have gone far. He began to run. At a junction the lines of cars waited behind traffic lights, ready to edge forwards, and people moved purposefully but blankly in all directions.

'Seen an old man, wearing a green coat?' he asked a woman wheeling a pram who shook her head. He ran on, suddenly afraid he was lost. Then he saw Rory, darkly filling a doorway and dashed across the road between the slow-moving traffic.

'Where you bin? You'll get lost.' Rory sounded annoyed. 'Next time I'll turn back. You keep up.'

'Sorry,' Driscoll muttered as they moved off.

They passed doorways with stacks of doorbells and windows where curtains half hid dark interiors. Driscoll wondered what sort of house his mother lived in. Did she sleep in a small bed like his? Where did she hang her clothes? Did she have friends to talk to? Tonight, he thought, when she came home he would tell her about the hive and she would help him cut the straws up the way she had helped him with growing the sunflower one year. He had got second prize and a book full of facts about nature. They used to play a good game with that book. He would ask questions like, How many teeth do chimpanzees have? and she would guess the answer. Then she used to ask him. They kept the score and he always won because he read the book at night and tried to remember all the facts: Grizzly bears live in North America. They eat salmon which they catch in rivers, and honey from the nests of wild bees.

Remembering the game, Driscoll hadn't noticed that Rory was no longer beside him. Turning back, he saw him transfixed, staring into a garden. Driscoll ran back and asked, 'What's up?' He found himself looking at a washing line of clothes.

'I could do with that,' Rory nodded at a blanket that lay on the ground beneath the line.

'What? That blanket? It's all wet. C'mon.'

'Fetch it for us, Driscoll. It's a good blanket.'

'No way. I'm not going in there. I might get caught.'

'It don't belong to no, one, does it? It's on the ground.'

'Rory! C'mon.'

'Get it for us and I will. Be a mate. We'll hide it. Get it later.'

Desperate to go on, Driscoll suddenly darted into the garden, scooped up the blanket and started to walk off down the road. He held it out at arm's length to prevent the moisture from soaking through his sweater. He could hear Rory breathing behind him. He expected at any moment a hand on his shoulder, an angry face peering down at him, but nothing happened. Two boys rode past on bicycles. 'What you got there then?' one called out to him. Rory came up beside him.

'Stick it in there Driscoll.' Rory nodded towards a bush in someone's garden close to the pavement. Driscoll pushed the blanket in among the earth and tangled roots.

'There.' He glanced around to check no one had seen him. 'I did it.'

'We'll get it later.' Rory looked satisfied. Driscoll felt a sense of achievement. He used to pretend at school that he nicked things, now he really had and it had been quite easy.

Just as Driscoll was despairing that they would never arrive, Rory went into an Underground station. People shrouded like chrysalises lay along the walls, incubating in the warm air that drifted up the escalators. A young woman stood playing the violin. She wore a woollen cap and her fair hair protruded from beneath it. Her skirt, red and yellow, sang out against the beige tiles. As they approached, she winked at them. Coloured beads shone against her brown sweater. Driscoll couldn't take his eyes off her. She was more beautiful than his mother, more beautiful even than Miss Trimmer.

'Lily.' Rory nodded towards her, took the piece of pie from his pocket and began to eat. Driscoll looked away. He wished he had eaten more breakfast. Since his mother left he had had school dinners, not packed lunches, and so now had nothing to eat. He listened to the music. Coins dropping onto the cloth at her feet knocked against each other, and the ticket barrier clicked continuously as people moved through it and down into the darkness below.

Exhausted by the walk and mesmerized by the music, Driscoll jumped when Rory put his hand on his shoulder and said, 'Lily's going to take us to where she's seen this woman. Lily this is Driscoll.' She smiled down at him.

'Hello Driscoll. I hope it's her. We'll have to see.'

As they walked away from the Underground he wished they would walk faster. Rory's slow pace annoyed him and he wanted to go on with Lily, leaving him behind to wait for them.

'It was a bit muzzy, that photo,' Lily said. Driscoll walked between them.

'She could be tired of kids talking all day,' Rory said to Lily over his head.

'I don't talk all the time.' Driscoll glared up at Rory, suddenly angry. 'She'll want to see me. She'll be missing me.'

'Course she will,' Lily said. 'This woman, the one who may be your mum comes to a café around lunch time. I've seen her several times. She's small and dark, sometimes wears a check coat.'

Driscoll couldn't remember a check coat but thought it might be new.

'The café's close now.' Lily moved her violin case into her left hand and put her right hand on Driscoll's shoulder. They stopped walking. She pointed across the road. 'See that café Driscoll? There she is, she's there at the table on her own, and she's wearing that coat. Do you see her? Is it her?' He looked through the traffic, and through the window behind which huge people sat awkwardly at small tables, and at a woman wearing a check coat. He abruptly swung around to face Lily and Rory.

'It isn't her. That's not my mum. You got it wrong. It isn't her.'

'I said it mayn't be her, didn't I?' Rory muttered.

'He's disappointed, it's only natural he should be.' Lily moved towards Driscoll who shrugged her away.

'Leave me alone. That's not her.'

With his hands in his jeans pockets he walked away from them into a doorway where he leant, his back to the street, against the wall. Tears blurred the edges of the blue tiles on the floor. He kicked the door. Lily's skirt swept, red across the blue, as she squatted down beside him.

'I'll keep looking Driscoll. We both will. I'm sure we'll find her some day. Don't cry now.'

'It's not fair.' He kicked the door again. 'It should have been her.'

'Why don't you come back, and see me . . . we'll look together . . . I'll give you a go on my violin . . . you can see where I live . . . would you like that?' Driscoll nodded. 'Listen, Rory wants to get back, to get his pitch for the night.' He nodded again. 'He's worried about losing it. You know where to find me? In the Underground. I'm nearly always there, in the mornings.'

'Move yourselves.' A man carrying a parcel pushed between them and slid his key into the lock. Lily took Driscoll's hand as they moved off to follow Rory who had started to walk back along the street.

Driscoll ate the sandwich that Lily had made for him before they left her, and wandered along behind Rory. The excitement of the day had faded, like the sun, which was now lying low in the sky. The street lights were on, awaiting the darkness which had begun to seep around the houses and among the evening traffic. He looked into the Underground station, a young man stood in Lily's place, playing a harmonica. Out of the corner of his eye, he spotted across the road an advertisement for his favourite car and, as he lowered his eyes, there, standing at a bus stop, beside a man, was his mother.

He darted across the pavement and stepped out onto the road shouting, 'Mum, Mum, it's me!' A car hooted and a woman shouted out of the window at him. He looked frantically along the road to left and right for a pedestrian crossing and shouted to Rory, 'It's her, I've seen her. Wait, Rory it's her.' He raced towards a set of traffic lights calling out, 'Mum it's me! Wait!' A man stepped aside saying, 'Take it easy son.' Driscoll stood by the lights waiting, his heart pounding. A line of buses crept one behind the other, close to the pavement towards the lights. He could no longer see his mother.

Rory stood watching as he sped across the road in front of the stationary traffic. He turned towards the bus stop and stopped: there was no one there. Realizing that she must be on one of the buses which were now moving slowly away, he ran along beside them trying to see in the windows and calling out, 'Mum it's me Driscoll! It's me, wait, wait!' Then, as if pulled by some magnetic force, all the buses began to accelerate. Driscoll stood watching them uncertain what to feel. He had seen her, so she did live round here, but now, second by second, she was being carried into the distance away from him.

Rory waved and beckoned to him and, slowly, he re-crossed the road and went up to him.

'It was her, it was. She's in one of those buses. She didn't see me.' He looked questioningly at Rory as if he might have a solution.

'You know she's around 'ere now don't yer? Makes it easier eh? You could come back, 'ave another look, bring your Dad, eh Driscoll?'

'Yeah, but . . . I wish she'd seen me Rory, I wish she had. I . . .' He could feel the tears coming into his eyes again. 'I . . . Rory . . . eh, I've got an idea. Hang on, I wanta get something.' He dashed into a newsagents and emerged some minutes later clasping a black felt tip, the sort that didn't rub off, the sort Miss Trimmer used at school. All the way back, along the roads, across the squares, by the bush hiding the blanket, Driscoll drew arrows. He drew them on walls, bus stops, posters and litter bins and as he drew, he grew happier and happier. Tomorrow he would return, tomorrow he would see Lily again, tomorrow they would bring his mother home.

They collected their bags from the café. Driscoll told Patsy about their day. 'Lily's great. She's terrific on the violin, really good and tomorrow I'm going to see . . .'

'Come on, Driscoll.' Rory stood by the door, the newspapers under his arm and the carriers at his feet.

'I'm telling Patsy. I saw her, I did, she's okay and . . .'

'I've gotta get a box for the night.' Rory opened the door letting in cold air.

'Bye Rory. See yer,' Driscoll called. 'Lily's gonna teach me how to play.' Rory manoeuvred himself through the door and out into the street.

By running fast Driscoll managed to arrange himself along the sofa in front of the television before his father returned. He wanted to jump up and shout, 'I've seen her, I know where Mum is,' but seeing his father's tense face, he decided to leave it for a little while anyway. When his father settled down to watch the news he went into the kitchen, collected the bundle of straws and, sitting on the floor at his feet, began measuring them, carefully cutting each one, ready for the hive he would start making at school tomorrow.

John Wakeman

John Wakeman was born in 1928 in London where
he has worked as a librarian. He later moved to
New York where he began to work as a freelance
journalist and editor. His publications include
World Authors, 1950-1970 and *1970-1975; World
Film Directors, 1890-1985* (2 vols); and *A Room for
Doubt* (selected poems). He has written for radio
and television and published poems, essays and
reviews in Ambit, Encounter, The New
Statesman, The New York Times, The Observer,
The Times, TLS, etc. He is co-founder and
co-editor of The Rialto poetry magazine. This is an
excerpt from his semi-autobiographical novel.

Ticktack

*J*ack spends part of his working-class childhood in Edward James's house in Wimpole Street. Edward James (1907-1985), reputedly a bastard of Edward VII, was a millionaire and an early collector of the surrealists. His London house, emptied during the War, retained traces both of the surrealist movement and of his passion for the dancer Tilly Losch, from whom he was scandalously divorced. Jack is a fatherless writer; Edward a childless patron: both bastards, probably

one

I was sitting in the jungle on a slab of yellow concrete. It was part of a wall, and five rusty rods splayed from the unfinished end holding a cat's cradle of ivy.   Half-way along the top rod a bloody great butterfly tensed motionless, as if about to spring. Its wings were easily a foot across, dark blue shot with pale green, like sometimes oceans are.

The butterfly made me nervous. I know that's silly, but I get nervous quite easily. That doesn't mean that I never do anything rash; on the contrary. But I can't, for example, go into the Woolworths in Finchley High Street without getting jumpy, thinking that everyone will think I'm going to nick something and that I'll be collared by the store detective and find that I've actually got a Mickey Mouse watch in my pocket, still in its plastic box.

That's one of the reasons why I always walk around with my hands in my pockets. Jo says that this habit, and my nose, and the stoop I affect to disguise my impressive height, make me look like a well-gorged old mosquito. She says this affectionately.

That afternoon I was not in Woolworths but all alone in the Mexican jungle, where anybody might be nervous. Except Tarzan, of course. A hang-up about Tarzan is among the numerous things I had in common with Edward James. In order to get him into Eton they sent him to a horrible crammer in East Grinstead and he told all the other little rich boys that at night he flew secretly to Africa and conversed with apes. They were so stupid that they believed him and so corrupt that they reported his truancies to the shit who ran the place. Edward was sent to Coventry for a month, which must have been a nasty change after Africa.

In point of fact, this Mexican hillside looked quite different from the jungle in the Tarzan movies. It was quiet and respectable and rather dark, like an English church on a weekday. Even the big ferns and wild orchids suggested an exotic experiment left over from the annual flower arranging competition.

There were thick lianas dangling like bell ropes from some of the trees for Tarzan to swing about on if he fancied it, but no sign of chimpanzees or lions or charging elephants. Nor had I seen any people since Canello dropped me at the foot of the hill a couple of hours earlier. There was a ruined temple in one of the Tarzan pictures, but never anything like the surreal follies Edward had built in his jungle.

The folly where I sat brooding was called The House Destined to be a Cinema. I only knew this because someone, presumably Edward himself, had painted its name in big dots like black neon lights over the doorless doorway. The place was shaped like a figure eight, with bulbous curved walls in thick yellowish concrete which had been scored with wavy horizontal lines.

I finally worked out that it was supposed to look like a giant peanut shell, but it wasn't easy. For one thing the building was not finished. There was no roof and in places, like the bit where I was sitting, the walls were only a couple of feet high and already grown over and cracked by ferns and creepers and thin young trees. It didn't really need a roof because the bigger trees all around met high overhead, with just glimpses of blue sky peepboing through the shifting branches.

There was an Arab proverb that Edward liked to quote, or so I had read: *You should never finish building your own house.* He certainly hadn't finished building this one, or any of the others I had seen. They were scattered all up this hill he had bought in the Sierra Madre, and I had no idea what most of them were meant to be. There was a thing like a Greek temple and a fifty-foot concrete sunflower and a Tarzan treehouse and something resembling the skeleton of a whale. The House Destined to be a Cinema was about half-way up the hill, and that was quite high enough for a man of fifty-eight in imperfect health.

My feet were cold. Sentimental as ever, I had taken off my socks and trainers and got into Edward's espadrilles, what was left of them. The rope soles were frayed and matted into leathery slabs, and my rather beautiful toes poked out through the shredded canvas tops. I didn't know the time, because my old Elgin had died on the flight from Miami to Tampico, but it was beginning to feel late.

Who was The House Destined to be a Cinema destined for? The peasants who had built it? The flora and fauna? Edward himself in lonely splendour? The movies were another interest we had in common. He had never been in the trade like me, of course, but he did once act in a film, and when he was very small he liked to pretend that he was a movie camera. When something moved or excited him he would say *tick*, switching himself on to record the scene forever. When it was over he would say *tack*.

It's time to say *tack*, I thought. I had come all this way to talk to him about our lives, but he had eluded me. I had come all the way from the dumbwaiter at 35 Wimpole Street to this purpose-built ruin in the jungle, a journey of forty-five years. All the way from Heathrow to Miami to Tampico, and a hundred and fifty miles on the stinking buses to Xilitla, and then fifteen more miles in Edward's big yellow Nash to this quiet hill.

Soon Canello would be here with the Nash to return me to Xilitla, and then I would be on my way back to Finchley and Jo and Charlie, poorer but no wiser. Nothing learned, nothing changed, nothing gained.

The butterfly twitched and made me jump. It flickered its great blue sails, and then started tilting them at various experimental angles, like a windmill feeling for the wind. The wings were so big that they actually made a draught and I shivered. Perhaps I was in shock. I got the half-bottle of Gordon's out of my flight bag and took a prophylactic pull on that, and lit a fag off the stub of the last one. There was already quite a pile of stubs on the wall beside me: Jack's funeral pyre, Jo would have called it.

Looking down at my long pale toes, cradled in the ancient ruins of Edward's espadrilles, I began to cry. I jumped up and tore the espadrilles off my feet and hurled them, one at a time, as far as I could into the jungle. One for my life and one for his.

That was too much for the butterfly. With an audible flap it lifted off, tumbling up like a piece of sky into the thin shafts of light that poked down through the trees. I missed it. It was the only blue around, because the fragments of real sky visible through the branches had gone coppery. Canello was supposed to collect me before nightfall, but perhaps he had forgotten or joined a circus or killed himself.

I went to the arched doorway and looked down the hill and, as I did, the black tops of the massed trees below me turned as if by alchemy to gold. I was shivering and hungry and crying and didn't know what I was ever going to do. No problem, because the fucking Mexicans had obviously left me here to die.

You should never finish building your own house. – Oh, Daddy, why? There was a crash in the jungle behind me and I swung round like a frightened cat. What had been a golden Technicolor twilight minutes before was now all green and misty Gothic gloom, the trees huddling together, the orchids shut down for the night, the ferns waving goodbye in a rising breeze. From behind the ferns a large white bird flapped slowly up, bearing in its long bill one of the espadrilles. It disappeared into the trees and night began.

two

I found the espadrilles at 35 Wimpole Street, in the walk-in safe in the butler's pantry. When I first explored the safe it seemed to be empty except for an ancient book printed in Latin and bound in vellum. The words meant nothing to me but I was fascinated by the pale smooth skin of the binding. After five hundred years, or whatever it was, you could still see the veins of the animal it was flayed from. Or I think you could. My memories of childhood are not very dependable.

The book was obviously valuable and I couldn't understand why it had been left in the unlocked safe. My mum thought it was a trap. She had been in service and explained that rich people often left around portable objects of value to test the honesty of their servants. For that reason we never took the book out of the safe, although we were not exactly servants in that house. Edward James, the owner, was in America, and my mum was the caretaker. She lived in the basement with my two grown-up sisters.

The house was new to me. Before the war, when my dad was still alive, they had a similar job looking after a big empty house in Oxford Square, near Marble Arch. One Sunday morning, getting up as usual to make the tea, Dad dropped dead of a heart-attack. I heard him fall and the Airedale barking and pulled the blankets over my head. At first they pretended he was only ill, and sent me to play with a sloppy child named Owen. I pondered the evidence all day and at teatime blurted out the opinion that my father was dead. Owen's mother told me not to show off.

I was ten when that happened, and afterwards everything went mad. The war started and the grammar school I had just joined was evacuated to the horrible town of Redruth in Cornwall. I naturally thought it must all be my fault. The Hitlerian masters terrified me and the boys bullied me and I was billeted with a monstrous old Christian hypocrite. She told me several times that my mum didn't love me because she didn't send her enough money. I said boldly that she didn't have any more money and did love me; but sometimes, thinking of friends who had been allowed to stay home in London, I was not sure.

While I was in Cornwall my mum lost her job in Oxford Square because my father had gone and there was no one to do repairs and things. By the second year of the war, when she finally gave way to my pleadings and let me come home for the summer holidays, she was the caretaker of 35 Wimpole Street.

By that time, the summer of 1941, the blitz was supposed to be over. Nevertheless, on my second evening at home the sirens started wailing at about eight o'clock. I'd heard sirens before, of course – practices and false alarms – but this was different. This was my own heroic city and I felt privileged and thrilled to be blitzed in it. My mum started chewing her bottom lip as she did when she was worried, and I thought that was a bit windy of her. Both of my sisters were out, Dorothy pursuing her love life somewhere and Madge on duty with the Auxiliary Fire Service.

Our air-raid shelter was the big safe in the butler's pantry. I helped Mum drag a mattress in there and fetched blankets and candles and things. She wedged the massive iron door open with a flat iron so that we would not be trapped forever by the door being blasted shut. The safe was very large but most of the space was taken up by deep shelves. There was just enough room for the mattress and a chair for Mum.

I curled up on the mattress with the old book, trying to guess what the words meant and to imagine the people who had printed it. For some reason I thought of them as monks in a big dark room with sunlight coming in through narrow windows. All the time I was listening. Mum was reading some novel.

After a long time we heard a small bang and then a long drumroll of them. I looked up, grinning with excitement, but Mum chewed her lip and shook her head. 'I hope the girls are all right,' she said. 'I expect they are.'

'Where's Dorothy?'

'She was going to the flicks with Rodney Darling. Up West.' Rodney was a rather posh fireman that Dorothy had poached from Madge. We called him Darling because he was liable to use such expressions.

'That's not the West End they're bombing,' I said reassuringly. 'They're too far away.'

'I know.' She did know, too, and I didn't. There had been no bombing in Redruth because it wasn't worth bombing. But I had read all about the blitz in the *Daily Express*.

Suddenly we could hear the steady groaning of aeroplane engines, then all sorts of bangs and plonks and rumblings.

'Listen to that,' I said. 'One of theirs. I bet it's a Junkers.'

'I don't know. I can't tell the difference.'

'That's a Junkers all right.'

The AA guns in Hyde Park started pumping away but the purposeful droning continued and grew louder. I thought about the men up there in the dark and cold, my enemies, who had come all this way to kill me but could not, and I was exhilarated. They were not real like my enemies at school. They were the sneering villains in a war film and it never occurred to me that they might enter my actual life and do me harm. Rolling on my back on the mattress, I aimed an imaginary machine gun up at them and gave them a long burst. In reply they dropped a single large bomb.

We listened to its long deepening whistle as it fell down and down and down for so long that I began to think it had passed us – had missed the spinning crust of the earth altogether. I stopped firing and sat up and looked at Mum. She made one of her faces, raising her eyebrows and pursing her lips into a smile of rueful complicity, as if to say: 'We're for it now.'

When the explosion arrived I didn't hear it but felt it, as if someone had clapped his hands violently over my ears. The house rocked like a cradle. 'Bloody hell,' I said, giggling. Then I saw Mum's face, her mouth open, terrified, and for the first time I felt fear myself. The light went out and in the dark Mum touched my arm. 'Jack,' she said, her voice shaky. 'Are you all right, Jack?'

'What's happened to the light? Have they hit us?'

'I don't think so. It must have hit the electric main.' She switched on the torch and by its light I lit a candle, surprised to see that my own hands were shaking.

The plane seemed to have passed over and it was quiet for a while. We smiled at each other in the gentle light of the candle. Then we heard the urgent bells of fire engines. One jangled right past our house, and you could hear its brakes squeal at the corner. I thought of my sister Madge, working the switchboard at the AFS station behind Baker Street, speaking in the efficient, affected voice she put on for the purpose.

'I bet that's Madge sending out the engines.'

'Maybe. I hope she's not worrying about us. That engine sounded as if it went just round the corner. I'd better go upstairs and see if there's any damage.'

'I'll come.'

'Oh no you won't. I should never have let you come home. They said the blitz was over.' She heaved open the door. It was pitch dark in the butler's pantry as well. Mum played the torch on the blackout curtains. 'At least the windows look okay. I'll just have a poke around upstairs. Then I'll make us a cup of tea.'

'Aren't you supposed to wait for the all-clear?'

'No, it's all right. You never get bombs striking in the same place twice.'

'Why can't I come with you then?'

'Because you can't. You stay in there and do as you're told.'

I was not used to her bossing me about. It would serve her right if I crept out behind her and followed the torchlight upstairs and made her jump. But I remembered how frightened she had looked and thought I'd better not.

The candle in its saucer was on the floor, and the safe began to fill with creepy shadows. I picked up the saucer and put it on the edge of one of the deep shelves where they used to keep the silver. By the flickering light of the candle I saw, in the deepest darkest corner, a heaving nest of rats.

The light steadied, and I could see that it was only a funny-looking pair of shoes. I pulled them out and found that they had rough string soles and navy blue canvas tops. They looked brand-new. I had grey school socks on but no shoes, and I pulled one of them on. It fitted me perfectly. Like Cinderella, I thought, then blushed because Cinderella was a girl. The all-clear began, like a long sigh of relief. Suddenly the lights came on in the safe and in the pantry. They flickered, went out, then came on again, sweet and steady.

There were no more raids while I was home and that was my most exciting night of the war. I felt brave. Even the sneering sods at school would have to be impressed when I got back. Back to Redruth: oh God, that day would come. If they had killed me it would never have come. If it had killed just me, not Mum! But that would probably have broken her heart. Oh bugger.

Maybe it would be different at school because I had been in the blitz and faced death. I would be changed; not a clumsy coward any more but strong and serene. Trevitt and Clegg, Harrison and Rixon, would sense the change and treat me with respect. No they wouldn't. Harrison would still call me Fatgut, though I wasn't really fat. 'Here listen,' he would shout, 'come and hear how Fatgut won the war.' Trevitt would twist my nose with one hand and rip my flies open with the other, screaming 'Blitzkrieg!'

That story of Parker's. He said he had found it in a train, but everyone knew he had written it because he was such a dirty sod. You could borrow it for a day and then you had to pass it on. It was about a bird in the French Resistance who gets captured by the Nazis, and this Gestapo bloke has her alone in his office tied to a chair. And she won't tell him what he wants to know so he starts unbuttoning her white blouse. I tossed off into my underpants and went damply to sleep in the safe.

I was still in the safe when I woke up. Mum was standing in the doorway with a cup of tea. Behind her I could see dusty sunlight sifting in through the barred window of the butler's pantry. I was too weak with happiness to want to sit up and just lay there grinning at her. She grinned back. We weren't really used to each other yet. She had come down to Redruth once but that had been a year ago and she looked older now. She's got a nice face though, I thought.

'Come on, Sprucer,' she said. 'I've got to go out. It's nearly ten o'clock.'

She had found me already asleep when she came down from her tour of the upstairs and had decided to leave me where I was. There had been no damage to the house. A two hundred pound bomb had come down around the corner in Weymouth Street. It had completely demolished one empty house – knocked it out like a tooth, Mum said and broken scores of windows. One old woman had had a heart attack, but by some miracle no one had been killed.

'That was good,' I said, though obviously it would have made a better story if there had been mass slaughter and blood pouring down the gutters. I asked about my sisters. Madge had sent a note round by one of the firemen saying that she had been on the switchboard half the night and was going to sleep at the

AFS station. Dorothy and Rodney had had to leave the cinema halfway through *Goodbye Mr Chips* and take shelter in Leicester Square Underground. She had already gone off to work. Dorothy was clever at figures and had a good job with the Ministry of Supply in Holborn.

Mum gave me my tea (real sugar) and a few minutes later came back in her old navy coat and navy straw hat, carrying her brown oilcloth shopping bag. 'I'm going to try and get some sausages for your dinner,' she said, 'but I'll have to queue. And then I've got to try to sort out about your ration book, so I might be a long time. Are you going to be all right?'

'Course I am.'

'Now remember what I told you. Don't, whatever you do, go upstairs.'

'But when am I going to see it?'

'I'll take you round when the time is right. But I told you, you're not even supposed to be here. No children. If the agent popped in and found you wandering about upstairs, I'd get the sack.'

'Yes. All right then.'

'You promise you won't go upstairs?'

'I promise.'

I heard the basement door shut and her trudging up the area steps and suddenly wished I had gone with her. Tomorrow I would. Finishing the tea, I found a film of brown sugar at the bottom of the cup and nibbled it slowly off the spoon. When I got up my feet felt funny and I realised that I still had the string shoes on. They must have belonged to the man who owned the house, this Edward James, and they must be pretty valuable to be in the safe.

The shoes were very comfortable and light. I went out into the passage, took a run, and jumped. I did it again and was sure that it was the longest jump I had ever done. Usually I was hopeless at games, but in these shoes I floated. It struck me that this was one of the things about being rich: you could afford special shoes that helped you do long jumps and it was probably like that with practically everything.

Edward James must have very small feet because the shoes fitted me perfectly. I wondered what he was like and what he was doing in America, leaving my mum to look after his house. She had heard that he was living in Hollywood and I knew what that was like. I had seen a film about it, a musical that had Anne Miller in it. She had to do this tap dance sitting down in a revolving chair and she had to pull her long skirt right up to the top of her thighs. I went along to the lavatory and tossed off and had a pee afterwards.

When I came out of the lav I felt scared. It was miles along the dark passage that went right through the basement to the garage at the back of the house, where the mews was. In the garage, up a little flight of steps, was a workshop with a proper bench and vice. Mum had showed it to me the day before and said I could do fretwork there with my old fretsaw. I didn't fancy going there alone, but at that time I was practising not being a coward. I set off along the passage, turning on lights as I went.

The games master had written in my report that I was timid. Trying to get braver, I had been going to see a lot of horror films in Redruth and then making myself walk home afterwards up Church Lane without a torch. Now I started remembering bits of those films, especially one where Emlyn Williams was a homicidal maniac who cut his throat at the end with a bit of broken glass.

The passage itself wasn't so bad. It was the doorways into little rooms and the wine cellar and the coal cellar. There were deep shadows in the doorways where a man could wait. I got to the garage and pushed the door open. Sun was shining weakly in through the dirty windows along the top of the big doors. It shone on a dark patch of oil in the middle of the floor, and it gleamed like blood. I turned and ran, too timid even to turn off the lights.

It felt all right in the kitchen. There was plenty of light coming in from the well of the house, and the room was warmed by an enormous Aga cooker. There was a set of carving knives in a pot on the dresser, all with handles made from antlers. I got out the biggest one and thought if anyone came after me he'd better watch out. I felt hungry and used the knife to cut a tomato sandwich. Mum and the girls had been saving up their rations for me, and there was more food in the larder than I had seen for years.

I washed my dirty hands and rinsed my face under the big brass tap in the stone sink. Now I had the knife I felt ready for anything. I went along the passage again as far as the garage and then strode back to the kitchen, flicking off the lights as I went. With the big knife as a cutlass, I had a sword fight, hacking and stabbing down half-a-dozen bemused opponents, leaping about like a lethal ballet dancer in my magic shoes.

Why shouldn't I go upstairs? What was so bloody special about Edward James's upstairs? There would probably be a locked room, wouldn't there, and inside, a row of rotting heads, oh yes, and the Bluebearded agent standing behind me when I turned in horror. Well, bad luck to him if he was, because I had the knife and I had the shoes.

I pranced out of the kitchen and through the green baize door into the butler's pantry. As a surprise for Mum I tidied up my bed and the safe, swinging the iron door shut with a clang. The open door had been hiding a hatch in the wall. Mum had called it the dumbwaiter. I had been struck by the word, but there were so many other things to take in that I had forgotten it. The hatch had a wooden frame like a picture, but painted cream. Where the picture should have been was a cream panel with a brass handle. I idly took hold of the handle and lifted, and the panel slid up.

Inside was a big box made of unpainted wood. There was a hole in the top at the left, and another one below it in the bottom of the box. Through the holes ran two thick ropes like bell ropes. I pulled cautiously on the rope nearest me. No bells rang but the whole box slid silently a foot or so upwards. I pulled on the other rope and the box came down again, a bit lower than before, so that there was a space above it. I fetched the torch and shone it up into the space. The box moved in a dark hole that went right up inside the building, like a miniature lift shaft. That's what the dumbwaiter was – not a mute servant like us, but a little lift to take things up and down from floor to floor of the house.

A frightening thought came into my head. The box looked just about big enough for me to get in. I pressed down experimentally with both hands on the floor of the box. It wobbled about a bit but did not sink at all, however hard I pushed. Jiggling the ropes until the box was just level with the sill of the hatch, I wriggled my body sideways into the box, last of all pulling in my feet. My head was bent onto my chest and I was all curled up like a hedgehog, but I was in.

The ropes were facing me. The box was a lot heavier with me in it, but when I pulled hard on the left-hand rope it moved upwards a little way. When I gave a panicky heave on the other rope, I came down again. I did it again, going up a bit further. The third time I went right up beyond the hatch and was in total darkness, rocking ever so slightly on the ropes. Instead of being scared I felt oddly safe, curled up there in the black belly of the house and trying to imagine what lay above me.

Mum had made me promise not to go upstairs, but this wasn't stairs. I let myself smoothly down to the hatch and jumped out, blinking in the light. There were the torch and the knife. I put them in the corner of the dumbwaiter and climbed in after them, my heart pumping furiously. I pulled strongly with both hands on the left-hand rope and disappeared.

three

Edward James suffered from a complex of space, or so Dali said.

When Edward was three, the family wintered in a villa they had rented at San Remo. On the way they spent a few days in Paris. They went by Channel steamer and train, and took so many servants that they half-filled the train.

One evening in Paris, Edward's nurse took him for a toddle in the Tuileries gardens. He had a purple balloon the colour of a grape. It was on a long string but the nurse, very foolishly, had not tied it to his wrist.

They reached the Louvre just as the declining sun transmuted the great creamy palace into gold. Edward was so astonished that he let go of his balloon.

It drifted up over the Louvre, higher and higher and smaller and smaller, and Edward began to cry. What made him cry was not losing the balloon, nor what his nurse would say to his mother and his mother would say to him. It was the idea of the balloon going on and on alone, into less and less of anything, for ever. As he said, it was a 'terror of the infinite'.

When he was grown-up, Edward once dreamed that he was on a mountain path that led up to a beautiful walled city. Higher up the mountain there was another city, and beyond that more cities, all the way up to the moon. Edward asked Salvador Dali to put this dream into a mural for the front hall of West Dean, his house in Sussex. Dali listened in silence to the dream, then looked at him darkly and said: 'Edward, you suffer from a complex of space.'

When Dali did the mural, he added an image of his own: two men are trying to control some horses, but one is plunging and rearing so violently that a man is being flung to the ground.

Edward does not seem to have minded Dali adding that bit of Freudian violence to the mural. It obviously made it a much livelier composition. All the same, it seems an outrageous intrusion, putting an idea out of your own head into someone else's dream. We all do it, though.

.

Edward woke up in his bedroom at West Dean and called for his nanny. She did not come. He heard someone walking very very quickly past his door and called again, but there was no reply. Someone else rushed past the other way.

The curtains were still drawn, so the room was quite dark. Edward climbed out of bed and used his potty, then got back in again. He heard Mary the parlourmaid shouting something in a low excited voice and someone downstairs answering.

His father had read him a story about a flying carpet and he pretended that his bed was that carpet. He turned over onto his stomach and spread out flat so as not to fall off. Holding tightly onto the edges, he closed his eyes and whispered, 'Up, up and away.'

The carpet had pink roses on it like the big one downstairs in his mother's drawing room, so first Edward flew quite low over the rose garden. He had to go higher to lift over the brick wall of the vegetable garden and higher still for the stables. He stopped the carpet and reached carefully out and felt all over the heavy golden cockerel on top of the weather vane. It was windy and the carpet rippled under him. Edward turned the squeaking weather vane so that it was pointing the wrong way. It was a kind of lie that made him laugh.

John Wakeman

Edward flew slowly around the steeple of the church, stroking the worn old stone. A pigeon landed on the carpet and he stroked that too, wriggling on his tummy and thinking about the delicious differences between stones and feathers.

Nanny came in almost running on her short legs. She flung back the curtains with a clatter. The sky was all grey. 'Master Edward,' she said, 'listen my love. We've got to be specially good today and very quick and very quiet. Because . . . guess what?'

'What? Is Daddy coming home?'

'Better, my love. The best ever. The King is coming to see us.'

A lot of the stories his father read to him had Kings in them. He knew what they wore and how powerful they were and about their good sons and bad sons. It made him feel anxious.

The King was a long time coming and Edward had a bad day waiting for him. The servants were excited and cross and everything seemed mixed up. His mother was nowhere to be seen. It began to rain during the morning, and rained all through lunchtime and into the afternoon.

When the King arrived, Edward was playing, alone and unnoticed, in the oak gallery above the front hall. He was sitting on the floor right up against the carved balusters, twitching his nose and pretending to be a rabbit in a cage. Suddenly, there was a great commotion downstairs and, through the open front door, Edward saw a long black car pull up with a drooping wet flag on the front. Behind it were other black cars. The chauffeur of the first car jumped out and opened the door and a big stout man stepped out and strode into the hall. He had no crown on, only an ordinary billycock hat, and he had pale thin eyes and a grey beard with a cigar stuck in it. A lot of other people crowded in behind him and Edward knew, with relief and disappointment, that this was the King.

Farley the butler came out of the drawing room carrying a silver tray with a glass on it and a pair of scissors. Behind him walked three footmen carrying an enormous cardboard box. There was one footman holding the back of it and one on either side and it reminded Edward of when the coachman died and a lot of men carried his coffin out of the church. Only this box was white, and tied with a fat pink ribbon. *Tick* went Edward.

Farley bowed to the King and murmured something that Edward could not hear. The King looked at Farley and lifted his eyebrows and looked at the box. He took the cigar out of his mouth and picked up the glass from the tray and drained it in one swallow. The footmen stepped forward and swung the white box up on end in front of the King. He took the scissors from Farley's tray and cut the ribbon which flopped onto the floor. The footmen eased the lid off the box and laid it aside. Standing in the box was the biggest doll that Edward had

122

ever seen. It had painted cheeks and lips and a white frilly blouse and layers of coloured skirts over white stockings.

In the side of the box was a key like the one in Edward's toy train, but a hundred times bigger. The King spoke to one of the men with him and everyone laughed. He stuck the cigar in his mouth and took the key in both hands and turned it. Then everything was silent in the hall, and in the silence a musical box began to play a little tune.

The doll jerked. Jerkily it stepped right out of the box and, taking its skirts in its hands, it jerkily began to dance. The music went faster and so did the dance. Edward could hear the doll's white shoes clack on the marble floor. It jerked its arms above its head and stamped and turned, and the flounced skirts twirled higher and higher about its legs.

The tune ended and the doll stopped. It bent its legs and sunk into a low curtsey. The King clapped heartily and so did all the people with him. As the doll lifted its painted eyes to the face of the King, Edward saw that they were his mother's eyes. *Tack.*

.

Just before he went to Eton, Edward's mother came to him and warned him about homosexuality, though at the time he had no idea what she was talking about.

It happened late one evening. Edward was in his room reading, for the umpteenth time, *Tarzan of the Apes.* He had just got to the part about the apes breaking into the Greystokes' cabin when his door flew open and there was his mother in her white dressing gown of quilted satin.

Edward jumped up in alarm, still holding the book. She had obviously been to bed, worried herself into a panic and got up again. Her face was flushed and shining with grease. Through her white lace bedcap Edward could see that she had left off her wig and was almost bald. She skidded to a halt and stared at his book.

'Edward.'

'Yes mother?'

'What book is that?'

'It's only *Tarzan.*' He held the book out to her, one finger in his place. She nodded dismissively and looked vaguely around the large, rather bare room, as if she was not sure how to proceed. Tightening the belt of her dressing-gown she went over and perched on the arm of Edward's chair, patting the seat for him to join her. Embarrassed and apprehensive, he sat down as far from her as the chair allowed.

'Edward.'

'Yes mother.'

'You're twelve years old.'

'Thirteen.'

'I know. It's only three weeks until you go off to Eton.'

'Two weeks and four days.'

'Please don't interrupt me.'

'Sorry.'

'Edward, you must be very careful there. Do you understand me?'

'Careful about . . . what? Doing prep and things?'

'Well, that, of course. But no. I mean the other business. You must be very careful of certain boys. Bigger boys.'

'Why?'

'You must be on your guard in case you are . . . assaulted in any way. In one way in particular.'

'Bullied do you mean, Mother? What particular way?'

'I'm sure you will find no bullying at Eton, but it is said . . . There may be some boys lower than bullies, depraved monsters who may try to rob you of your innocence. Of your illusions.' To Edward's horror, large tears began to slip down his mother's shiny face and off her chin onto her dressing-gown. 'Let me make myself absolutely plain,' she went on doggedly. 'I speak of monsters like the four great monsters of history. And if I say their shameful names, you will understand me.'

'Yes, Mother.'

'Very well then.' She looked at the wall: 'Nero.' She looked at Edward: 'Benvenuto Cellini.' She hesitated and, fumbling in the pocket of her gown, produced a scrap of paper, read what was on it, and nodded to herself: 'Heliogabalus.' She lowered her voice and glanced over her shoulder: 'Last and greatest. I mean the greatest monster. Oscar Wilde.'

She sighed with relief, put away the piece of paper, found her handkerchief and dried her eyes. She patted Edward on the shoulder and stood up, again staring around the room. 'We must have this room repapered while you are at school.'

'Thank you, Mother.'

'You must remind me.'

'Yes.'

'I'm glad that we were able to have this talk. Think about what I have told you.'

'I will. Yes. Thank you.'

Edward went to bed confused and anxious. To his many fears of Eton was added a new but nameless one. What illusions might he lose? What illusions did he have?

Robert Whittaker

After working for six years as a management
consultant in Europe and the UK, Robert
Whittaker turned to writing full-time. He has a
degree in modern languages from Cambridge.
Although a true Londoner, he has travelled
extensively abroad. He now lives in Canterbury.
He appears in print for the first time here with a
ghost story.

Old Man

It was good, no question about that: only twenty pounds a week for a large room, plus a bathroom all of his own and the use of the kitchen downstairs if he wanted it. The old man was a bit funny, but not unusually so. When Martin's grandmother had been that age she had acted strangely, and he was used to it. He had lived alone with her.

He stood in the room and mentally rearranged it. The desk would be best facing a wall, not by the window as it was now, If he sat there he'd just end up watching all the people go by, and that annoyed him, irrelevant people disturbing his concentration, people in the streets like flies in the air, people with big egos, small minds and grotesque mannerisms. He smiled, a little self-consciously at these thoughts and almost turned round to see if someone – the old man – was watching him and might guess them. It was funny, he wasn't like that normally; he had a sense of humour, but not a terribly coherent or articulate one, and he was never self-conscious, even at large gatherings.

His thoughts drifted back to the room. The armchairs would go along the side wall, the table by the window, the wardrobe – ah, that might be why he felt self-conscious: there he stood, reflected full-length in the mirror on the door of the wardrobe that lurked in the gloom by the door. He didn't enjoy seeing himself that clearly: he'd hang a coat or dressing-gown over the mirror. The wardrobe was too heavy for one person to move, and he had the feeling that the old man might not like the furniture moved around too much – though he hadn't even offered to show Martin around, just told him to go up and see for himself. For a person of such age he seemed peculiarly invulnerable, as if he didn't care whether Martin took the room or not; yet his eyes had been fixed on Martin while they had been talking, fixed with great interest. It had been rather unnerving. In fact he didn't really like the old man, he decided: the similarity to his grandmother was altogether too disconcerting, and he had never been able to stay long in the same room with her without feeling that he was wasting his time.

But the room was good. Very good. Thick carpets, neutral wallpaper, few distractions. He could work in peace here. It was much better than what he had expected after entering the hall downstairs, with its peeling worn wallpaper, the dust in the corners and a suspicion of mould in the air. Why didn't the old man charge more? He could get thirty easily. Perhaps it was because they were on the dingy outskirts of town, a fifteen minute walk from the centre. Martin shrugged his shoulders and pouted to himself; then a thought struck him and he sat on the bed. It was old, but well-sprung. He stretched out full-length and rolled over a few times: warm, quiet, comfortable and spacious. For some reason that clinched it. He picked up a small pile of history books he had left on the desk and went down the dark, still staircase.

The old man hardly reacted to Martin's announcement that he'd take it. He seemed indifferent. Martin asked if there were any restrictions on guests or hours he had to be in by. No, he was told, so long as there was no noise. When did he want to move in? As soon as possible: he wanted to get some work done before term started. A moment later he stood on the pavement outside in the dusk, keys to the house in his pocket, as if he had never seen the room or met the old man. The latter had again shown curious trust or indifference in simply giving him the keys in exchange for his current address. He walked away elated, without even a glance at the exterior of his new home. The house remained watchful in the twilight, indistinguishable from the other terraced houses extending away on either side of it. A subdued play and intermingling of colours and textures in its brickwork made it look almost alive.

Martin was looking forward to moving in. Miriam would like the place. She was in her final year and would be busy, which would leave him free to work. She was just the sort of girl he needed at the moment: honest, reliable, and very affectionate. He no longer wanted the reassurance of many friends and acquaintances, as he had in his undergraduate days: now he felt more independent, he could control himself and start settling down to a steadier way of life, a career. Miriam, he knew, had a similar attitude. She was very mature for her age. These thoughts gave him great satisfaction and he dwelt on them on his way home.

Two days later he was installed at last in the room above the taciturn old man. Standing at the window, looking down in the sunset at the quiet street below with the odd pedestrian or car, he was aware of the mirror in the wardrobe behind him. It was such a tranquil evening that he remained at the window, letting the peace soak into him; until finally he seemed to wake and, going over to the wardrobe, took out his dressing-gown and hung it over the mirror. He could work here in comfort.

And work he did. Even the last seductive warm days of the dying summer could not lure him out before term began and Miriam came. He spent the week alternating between his desk, table and bed. He hardly ever met the old man, and received no social calls, so apart from one day when he went into town to do some shopping he saw practically no one. He was free. Sitting in his room his mind flew far away, he forgot the present and the future and saw only the past, becoming caught up in it and letting his daydreams run away with him. He spent three hours one afternoon daydreaming over a photo of a Byzantine axe-head in one of the library books he had out. At first he had passed it by after a brief glance, but then he had returned and let his imagination flourish on the curves of cold bronze. He tried to bring it and its maker's purpose to life, imagining it raised by brown hands into the ancient air, the sunlight darting off it, and the slow, perfect curve of its descent. What part had it played in the events he read about every day? How many defeats and triumphs in death had it seen? But he came to himself later on, angry at having wasted the afternoon dreaming over a photograph. The trouble was that this was no isolated incident. He achieved little for all his reading, and the sensation of freedom vanished.

He was glad when term began, bringing with it a party, a few old friends and, of course, Miriam. He enjoyed the party, to which she was not invited. He had returned in triumph to do a doctorate. He knew the town, the university, the lecturers. He was experienced. He enjoyed this brief sortie into the outside world in the knowledge that afterwards he could return to his work and continue being a retiring academic. But when he actually arrived back at his room he was in a bad mood: he felt oppressed by the silence, his ears rang, and he wanted to be violently sarcastic towards someone, anyone. The only object he could find for this anger was a photo of Miriam. He picked it up and silently taunted it, debasing and insulting her until quite suddenly he no longer wanted to and felt mildly alarmed with himself. What was this mood? There was nothing wrong with her, or with him. He was perfectly content.

The following day Miriam came to see him at his place for the first time. He felt oddly nervous. She sat on one of the armchairs and asked him what he had done since they had last seen each other. Her interest and love quietened him. He felt somehow guilty and avoided her eyes as he handed her a cup of coffee. She didn't like the room, but it didn't matter as, later, she slept beside him, breathing lightly, her face calm and open as it always had been.

The day after that he was unable to concentrate on his work. It seemed unusually noisy outside, though he couldn't pin it down to anything specific. He was also strangely aware of the old man being in the house, having met him while coming in from shopping in the morning. He had received a mirthless questioning look from iron-grey eyes beneath the bushy eyebrows. The old man seemed to be waiting for him to say something, or expecting something to happen. Contrary to his first impressions, he had realised that his landlord was not absent-minded or senile in the least. Still quite handsome in a lean way, he moved swiftly and without a trace of feebleness, and even the swift smile he had thrown at Martin had been extremely deliberate. He had been carrying a kitten by the scruff of the neck from the living-room to the kitchen, his other hand underneath it, supporting it. Going upstairs, Martin had heard the back door open and close, presumably the animal being told to get some fresh air.

Again he felt that self-conscious desire to laugh, sitting at his desk thinking about it. The kitten had been motionless in the old man's hands with their tendons like wires. Its eyes were large, dark, and round with fear. It stared helplessly as it was borne away. Even now he felt anger when he thought of those eyes, half of it directed at the old man, half at the kitten. There was something disgusting in its helplessness.

He screwed up the notes he was trying to make and threw them across the room. His anger promptly turned in on himself; the whole silent atmosphere of the room pressed in on him as he crossed it to pick up the paper and unscrumple it. He needed the notes, and there were nearly two pages' worth there. As he sat down again he looked round at something that he knew was there, but had not seen, and that had attracted his attention somehow. It was strange: he had looked a moment ago, yet he had not seen it. A woman sat facing him wearing an elegant old-fashioned grey suit, her legs crossed, her hands in her lap, looking at him impassively, long, slightly untidy black hair contrasting with her immaculate dress. Her gaze was not as impassive as he had at first thought. It was at once timid and accusing, timidity prevailing. Her eyes, set in a sad and weary face, seemed to look deep into him while not allowing him to see into them. He had an impression that they were glazed and flat, seeing through him, as if he were a window, to something brutal beyond. He was surprised, but not shocked. He felt a mild alarm (what was it she could see in him?) coupled with a much stronger feeling: hatred towards her; hatred which he knew she could feel like a hot wind in her face and to which she could not reply. And her inability to reply redoubled his loathing until he felt exhausted with the effort of loathing an innocent object, and looked away at the ground. When he looked up again she was gone.

The room suddenly wearied him with its infinite expanses of wall and eternally identical corners and angles. He went out for a walk to cool off. He wouldn't let the woman bother him. Already he was beginning to doubt whether he had seen her at all. His mind flitted from object to object, finally settling on work. It was going badly, annoying him more and more every day. If Miriam hadn't come yesterday he didn't know what he'd have done. It was like a slap in the face for him when his work didn't go well, he became irritable and depressed. Perhaps that was why he had seen the woman – there was no other reason. It had shaken him to see her suddenly appear like that, and again he felt a desire to be violently sarcastic to someone, anyone. If Miriam had been on the doorstep when he arrived back he would have been rude to her. As it was, he crept upstairs, afraid of seeing the old man again, and tried to work, without much success. It was not that he looked over his shoulder for that woman again, just that he couldn't concentrate and kept feeling that there were events taking place beyond his field of vision, events he had no part in but which concerned him intimately. A conversation was taking place between two people who were close to him and knew him well, yet he was not allowed to join in or even to listen.

He poured himself a whisky. It was the only alcohol he allowed himself in his room and he usually reserved it for guests, but now he felt like breaking his own rules for a change. He asked himself why he was having the whisky and could only answer: why the hell not? Did it matter? He went and sat by the window. People went past in the open air. He felt trapped within himself. Never before had he found being himself so irksome. He wanted to be someone else, his own thoughts and feelings were no longer enough. This room annoyed him but he had to work in it: it was ideal.

He idly picked up the top book of a dusty pile that he had found in the room and dumped on the table. *Vanity Fair; Our Mutual Friend* . . . What was this? A hard cover from which the inside had been ripped. It was called *Old Man*, and the author's name was not given. He looked through the others in the pile. None of them belonged to that cover. He had never heard of it. One of the remaining books was similarly disembowelled – a bible – and he wondered what had happened to them.

The books were all old. They reminded him of the rows of books in his grandmother's house when he had lived there for a year before she died. He remembered her telling him: 'Books are wonderful, Martin. When you read no one can hurt you. Look at all the things that have happened to me.' She had been widowed twice and of her three children one had died in the war, another – his mother – was an alcoholic, and the third a neglected spinster. 'But I've managed and I'm quite happy. Though of course you mustn't let them take over.' Then she had laughed, and he had felt, as so often, that he didn't really matter to her or to anyone. He was oppressed by the memory of her laugh and the shelves bearing row upon row of books.

The next day found him in a cheerful mood. A morning's work in the dull dark library relaxed and reassured him, and he recognised the melancholy of the day before for what it was: an aberration. In the evening he had arranged to go for a drink and a game of darts with some friends, and back in his room after the evening meal he hung a dartboard on the door of his room and had a few throws to get his hand back in: he didn't want to be thrashed. It went well, and he started looking forward rather more to the game in the pub. He was hitting doubles like he used to, and as his confidence came back he tried to get round the board in doubles. At the second attempt he got to 13, went to pull the darts from the board, and returned to the book on the floor which marked his throwing-line. He hit double 14, and felt sure he could get to 20. Then, as his arm swung forward and the shining bronze of the next dart left his hand, his heart took a tremendous leap. The figure of the woman stood there, sad and timid eyes staring at him, her arms hanging down by her sides, and a look of reproach on her face, which was bruised in several places. The dart disappeared through her and she slumped slowly to the ground; then she was gone again. Why had she returned? What had he done? He flung the last dart at the wooden door and threw himself heavily onto his bed. He felt no hatred, only loathing and pity but it had been so sudden, how could he stop himself?

He lay there for a while. There was a ring at the door. It was Miriam, unexpected.

He went with her to the pub, tried to play darts, but it was no use, his shots went everywhere. He ignored Miriam, and went home early, unable to talk, with no desire to drink. At the gate he paused and looked up. His room was dark and empty. Even here he felt like an intruder. He wanted to see Miriam and hurt her in some way. Furious and impotent he went to bed, lying on his back thinking for a long time before sleeping.

For a while the work went better. He managed to push everything else to the back of his mind, and life was as he had planned it. But secretly he awaited and feared the woman's next visit. He and Miriam were close, but never talked much. Sometimes he saw, as she lay next to him, that she was and always would be a complete stranger. She made tea, she smiled sweetly, and beyond that he hardly knew her. Once he was on the point of being obscurely rude to her; a sap of cruelty rose within him, but then it stopped and indifference reigned again.

He actually exchanged words with the old man during this period. In response to an enquiry as to how he was getting on he invited his landlord upstairs to see. The old man followed Martin upstairs, and when he saw Martin's room he turned his grey gaze towards Martin and, for the first time, smiled. 'This is how I used to have the room,' he said. 'The desk here, the chairs by that wall, the wardrobe by the door. How strange that you should arrange it all in the same way.' Yet something in his manner suggested that it was not strange at all. He stood above the desk and looked down at Martin's work. Then, and later when the man was going down the staircase with its faint, timeless light, Martin wanted to hurl something at the back of his landlord's head, make it cave in, see its owner collapse inertly on the ground, extinguished in a second like the woman. But instead, nothing happened. And in the nothing were the seeds of later events.

Summer had vanished now and the town was grey with autumnal rains and winds. Friends and acquaintances noticed that Martin was withdrawn. He seemed to lurk inside himself, hiding fearfully from the world inside a facade of behaviour and attitudes. He went out less and less, and spoke less and less when he did go out. People felt ill at ease with him because he himself seemed ill at ease with them. But if they could have seen him when he was alone! He was a mixture of confidence and silent sarcasm. In his room he defied the world. It made him separate and aloof. He stood at the window and laughed at the people going home in the rain huddled under their umbrellas.

Yet one day he too was huddled under an umbrella and walking alone to the market to cheer himself up a little, alone in the rain like a small island. He bought some fudge, vegetables and cheese, then leafed through a few books at a stall. The new paperbacks bored him. He preferred the old tattered books. One was coverless: the spine was laid bare. The title *Old Man* stood alone above the opening line. He was surprised. It was almost certainly the substance of the empty cover that he had found in his room. He paid twenty pence to the sullen stallkeeper and walked away with it. On reaching home he shook the rain off his umbrella, took off his wet shoes, brewed a cup of coffee and curled up on the bed to read his find having confirmed that it was indeed the text belonging to the cover he had found in his room. The title page was missing, and he could not find the name of the author anywhere. He lay there and read until it was dark, the rain still beating on the roof, read with mounting apprehension and involvement.

It began as a simple love story: a case of poor boy – the narrator – meeting rich girl, and the rich girl's even richer father disapproving. The rich father did his utmost to dissuade his daughter from the marriage, but to no avail. She married the narrator, and her father disowned and did his best to disinherit her. Until then her father's plaything, she became the plaything of her husband. He became disgusted with her because of her meekness. At the same time he grudgingly acknowledged a certainty in her that he could never break down or bypass in any way. She loved him, and her love had survived the shock of their marriage and the move into a small, uncomfortable house. His own love had not. He envied her. He wanted her to hate people other than himself, to love him alone, but he could never extract an admission of hate from her. As she showed her feelings more and more rarely, cowed by his demands, so he became more cruel. It was partially, but not entirely, drink. His drinking was itself caused by something else. It was the house they lived in: two-up, two-down, it left no time for thinking or caring, and it goaded the narrator into a frenzy. He felt trapped in it, but his wife could and did accept it. His only remaining amusement was to torment the creature who held him there. He began to hit her when she annoyed him, and she accepted it without a sound. Then one day he pushed her down the staircase in a fit of anger and her spine was damaged in the fall. She could talk in hospital, but did not contradict him when he said she had had an accident. Paralysed from the neck down, she died two weeks later. It always seemed odd to him that she could never lift her arms in those last two weeks to protect her face as he had so often seen her do at home – home, that eternal irony.

And now, wrote the narrator, *I am an old man, weary, as I have been since the first year of our marriage. To be old when you are young is to be accursed. Although I am still healthy and can expect to live long, I await the person who will strike me down in that room where I struck her so often. Now she is no more than a name to me: Sarah.*

Martin finished reading and rested his head on the bed. His last thought before falling asleep was: Who was the author?

He was woken by the doorbell. It was Miriam, coming at the prearranged hour of nine which Martin had totally forgotten about. They went for a drink. Martin didn't trust himself to say anything. At the moment he could hardly take himself seriously. They were walking side by side and suddenly Miriam turned to him and said, 'What's the matter?' Her voice shook slightly. Her long black hair seemed slightly dishevelled, her face even whiter than usual. He wanted to hide, to be cold or sarcastic. Instead he stroked her hair and said, 'Nothing.'

'Yes there is.' She pulled away. 'You're ignoring me. We don't see each other often, at least not as often as I'd like, and when we do you treat me like a nuisance.' Her voice had risen. 'What's wrong. There is something wrong, isn't there?'

'No, of course not . . . only the landlord, he irritates me. I'm fed up with the work . . . ' It was no use. She was looking at him and he could see disbelief in her eyes. He walked on. It would be a waste of time trying to explain, he had nothing more he could say.

A few evenings later he was wandering home after a few drinks. His mind was free from the troubles of the last weeks and he walked slowly but steadily through the streets that led from the centre of the town to the outskirts. After a while he realised that there were other footsteps behind him, small and light and hard, a tap-tap like a woman's heels moving quickly with smaller steps than his. He knew at once who it was: the woman from his room. Their third meeting. The dark roads, lined by towering terraced houses, seemed to be a maze without an entrance or escape, its implacable walls hemming him in on all sides. The houses watched, the street lamps flickered in an unpleasant wind. He slowed right down and stared doggedly ahead, refusing in spite of his tension to look around. For the first time he noticed the light rain that was chilling him. The steps came closer and closer behind him, and he tensed himself to turn and confront the pale, bruised face and sunken eyes that followed him so. As they came close up to him he spun round: it was a small black boy carrying a toy boat. The boy's eyes were large and white in his face. He looked surprised and a little anxious, and stopped walking, but he was not afraid. His bare arms clutched the boat to his chest, and he looked up at the swaying, half-drunken monster in front of him.

Martin stared. For some reason this puzzled but fearless face increased his tension. What should he do? He stared into the small innocent face of the boy and saw himself, years ago, following his drunken mother through the streets, ignored and pushed away. He felt himself becoming abominable and cruel. A fear grew within him like a small mushroom that the boy would turn into something else something he was afraid to see, something he knew. His hand was hurting. He looked down and saw his knuckles white and wet, shining brightly in the lamplight, and the horror within him grew. He raised his hand to strike the child who stood there expectantly, wide-eyed – it was wonder in those eyes – and then he realised what he was going to do: his eyes dropped to the toy boat, he lowered his fist and turned and walked away. The boy stared after him as the rain came down harder.

The house, when he arrived back, was totally dark. He entered after just a moment's hesitation. In his room the dressing-gown had fallen from the wardrobe mirror. He picked it up angrily and jammed it hard over the mirror again.

He dreamed deeply. Earlier that week he had seen a pale woman with long black hair leaving a disco in the high street with a man, arm-in-arm, and had mistaken her for Miriam for a moment. Now he dreamed that it was Miriam, walking straight past him, laughing with the man until she saw him, then smiling secretly. She hated him as much as he hated her. He was right to hate her. She deserved it.

Soon it would be too much, he decided the next day. He was worried by the way he wanted to escape into the world his mind created. Maybe the woman he expected to see at every moment, with every turn of his head, was just a creation of his imagination. He awaited his third meeting with her avidly. True, he was a little nervous, but it was nervous excitement, not fear. The old man had invited him to have a cup of coffee for the first time today. That was a good sign – or a bad sign perhaps – at least a sign, he hoped. He sat in the room whose furniture he had rearranged so painstakingly, feeling tired and out of control. Something was breaking out of him, taking shape and threatening him.

It was in fact the beginning of the end, he realised afterwards, when the old man invited him into his living room for coffee. It was neatly furnished in Edwardian style, a little shabby but pleasant enough. There was a whisky decanter on the sideboard. The television seemed an anachronism. It was the beginning of the end, because he was invited again, and again, and became used to the alert, invulnerable eyes staring at him over the dining table, the grey eyebrows and old lips. He never seemed able to turn down an invitation to coffee. Every time he came the level in the whisky decanter had changed. Yet their conversations were banal: the weather, the town. Martin would some-times reveal a few of his plans, and the old man would listen in silence, nod-ding, a smile on his face. Occasionally he would talk about his past, but only about jobs and trivial incidents.

One day he spoke of his wife; and from a drawer in a dark corner of the room he pulled out a photo and handed it to Martin, who had to hold back a cry of recognition. This, then, was the third meeting. A well-cut suit, long hair, a beautiful, already slightly morbid face with eyes that looked into him even from a photo, but into which he could not look. The woman. 'Died over thirty years ago,' he heard the voice continue. 'Her father didn't want us to get mar-ried. Now she is no more than a name to me: Sarah, her name was.'

Now she is no more than a name to me: Sarah.

Martin turned and looked at the old man, and once more could have sworn he was being mocked by the expression in those eyes. In that moment he de-cided he would move out soon, the next day. He had no wish to live with the narrator of that story. The other dropped his gaze. Martin mumbled an excuse, and, as he left the room, he could feel the old man's eyes on his back.

That night he found his old camping knife and put it under his pillow. He lay in bed and thought of the time when he could laugh and joke with Miriam. Why had they become so distant? He had wanted to care about her. He had wanted to work well, control himself, sort out his life and see the future emerg-ing ahead of him like a path for him to tread. Instead he could only see the en-trance to a maze that ran between terraced houses and shadowy figures from the past. But he would not become like the hateful old man. He would not hurt Miriam. As soon as he had moved he would go and see her, explain and apologise. He would work hard, he would study history that remained where it belonged, in the past. He was determined.

He had had several whiskies before falling asleep, and perhaps it was those that gave him such unpleasant dreams. The first he could remember was again of Miriam walking past him on the arm of a man, laughing and shouting drunk-enly, her face made-up with lipstick, mascara, blusher . . . He raised the bronze Byzantine axe over her head, she laughed at him coarsely and he realised he could not hurt her. Then he was in bed. He sat up, sweating: by the light of the street lamps filtering through the thin curtains he could see the old man stand-ing in the room by the mirror. Where was his wife? Martin asked himself. Was she safe? And a desire to protect her welled up in him. He seized the knife under his pillow, pulled back the sheets and jumped out of bed. The hateful face of the old man was made up, his lips were clearly defined against his white face, his eyes were like black cave mouths. But then Martin, standing there trembling, saw the face of the black boy appear briefly in that of the old man: it was there, like a hill covered by mist or a man's face seen underwater. The eyes were soft and innocent. Martin raised the knife, his knuckles white, and brought it down on his enemy. It went through the face and splintered the glass of the mirror, the shock knocking it out of Martin's hands onto the floor. He turned to look for it and saw the dressing-gown on the floor by the half-open door, the whole room writhed and shook, he was within a mouth that echoed and vibrated with laughter, the dark staircase descended to a ravenous stomach, he turned again to see what it was that stood behind him just out of his range of vision . . .

He awoke.

The old man was indeed in the room, sitting by his bed, staring at him, smiling, his head nodding slowly.

Martin sat up, blood thudding in his ears, seized the knife under his pillow, and raised it, his hand shaking. The smiling face nodded on. The knife . . .

But Martin dropped it with a clatter on the floor. *I await the person who will strike me down and take from me the burden of living in this house.* He would not be the one. He remembered the woman, staring through him to something brutal beyond. He would not allow that brutality within him to triumph.

In the light filtering through the curtains he could see the smile leave the old man's face, which took on the look of indifference he had first seen on it.

As Martin placed the keys in the old man's hand the next morning and turned away for the last time, he thought he heard, from deep inside the belly of the house, a laugh.

UNTHANK

An anthology of short stories
with an introduction by Malcolm Bradbury £4.99

"The whole idea of a creative writing course seems perverse. How can it be creative if it is taught? And why should authors, that most notably anti-social of breeds, gang up together to trade tips late into the night? Yet the course at UAE has a distinguished track record. Set up by Malcolm Bradbury and Angus Wilson, it has nurtured such talent as Ian McEwan, and Ishiguro. This is the first anthology of short stories by recent participants . . . The topics are mixed, and if some of the contributions show a certain faltering, there are no obvious duffers. Given the prominence that the course has established, this is a kind of form-book of the names to watch."

THE SUNDAY TIMES

"These are, I think and hope, writers you have not heard the last of . . . as one of the students has said, it can be a burden as well as an opportunity to come into a course that now actually has a history and the pressure is on. But I think you will find that the writers here have risen to it."

MALCOLM BRADBURY

ISBN 0 9515009 0 2

Centre for Creative and Performing Arts